P9-CBG-068

Digging Up Secrets

Sandra Orchard

Annie's®

AnniesFiction.com

Digging Up Secrets

Library of Congress-in-Publication Data
Digging Up Secrets / by Sandra Orchard
p. cm.
I. Title
2017958114

AnniesFiction.com
(800) 282-6643
Victorian Mansion Flower Shop Mysteries™
Series Creators: Shari Lohner, Janice Tate
Series Editor: Shari Lohner
Cover Illustrator: Bill Bruning

10 11 12 13 14 | Printed in China | 9 8 7 6 5 4 3 2 1

1

Kaylee Bleu's part-time floral designer, Mary Bishop, burst into The Flower Patch, her white and gray hair wildly windblown, her complexion paler than the fistful of white lilies clutched in her hand. "Please tell me that hole in the side yard isn't what it looks like."

"What do you mean?" Kaylee's stomach lurched, then she realized what had Mary concerned. "George Bard is trying to locate the wellhead. He figures the foot valve in the bottom of the well is shot and that's why we have no water." And her plants were parched. She hurried toward one of the Victorian mansion's side windows to scope out her plumber's progress.

As she moved, she twisted her long, brown hair into a ponytail. It was a wonder it hadn't already turned as white as Mary's, despite the twenty years Mary had on her. At the window, Kaylee squinted down at the large, rectangular swath George had shoveled. She grimaced. He'd had to dig down almost four feet before finally locating the wellhead.

"Yikes, I didn't realize he'd have to dig so deep." Kaylee shook her head. "Wait, what did you think the hole was?"

"A grave!"

Kaylee shot Mary a frown.

Mary shrugged. "Hey, you can hardly blame me with the way trouble seems to find you."

A couple of the mysteries Kaylee had recently been roped into flitted through her mind, and she winced. "It's not as if I go looking for problems," she protested.

Mary squeezed Kaylee's arm. "I'm sorry. Chalk it up to too

many years as a police dispatcher before retiring to this job. Orcas Island may only have a few thousand year-round residents, but when our numbers swell during tourist season, some of the calls that come in would make your hair curl."

"Well please don't start any rumors about a body in my yard." Kaylee returned to the front of the store and flipped the sign to *Open*. "Chelsea Banks and her mother are due any minute to discuss what we can do for her wedding. And thanks to the crazy cheap package deals that new florist in Eastsound has been advertising, this might be the only wedding I do this fall." Kaylee stooped to straighten the royal blue bow tie her dachshund, Bear, sported proudly that morning. "I may have said I was looking forward to things slowing down with the end of tourist season, but just because it's September doesn't mean I want our business to dry up altogether."

Chelsea burst into the shop and Bear let out a happy bark in greeting. Grinning, Chelsea made a fuss over the little dog, while Mrs. Banks glanced around the shop. She appeared unimpressed.

"Welcome to The Flower Patch," Kaylee said cheerfully, trying to ignore the woman's sour expression. "I have the albums you asked to view set out over here." Kaylee motioned to a table at the back of the showroom stacked with albums showcasing designs from previous weddings. They featured her own arrangements as well as those of her grandmother, Bea Lyons, who had owned the shop before her but was now retired and lived in Arizona.

Mrs. Banks gave a nod and summoned her daughter to join her at the table. Chelsea oohed over picture after picture, pointing out aspects of various settings she'd like to include in her wedding, commenting on preferred colors, and asking the names of flowers that caught her eye.

A holler from the direction of the backyard sliced through the windows.

"What was that?" Mrs. Banks demanded haughtily.

Visions of George tumbling into the hole and injuring himself streaked through Kaylee's mind. "I'm not sure. Would you excuse us a moment?" She raced out the back door with Mary on her heels. The scent of ocean breezes and damp earth did nothing to slow Kaylee's racing heart as she spotted George scrambling out of the hole, clawing at the dirt like a wild man, his welding helmet bobbing on the top of his head.

"Are you okay?" Kaylee asked.

"Did you burn yourself?" Mary added, scanning his arms.

He flung off his helmet. "There's a body down there!"

"Of course there is." Kaylee glared at Mary. "Did you put him up to this?"

Mary was white again. Whiter than before.

Kaylee's heart sank. *Not a prank.* She vigorously shook her head. *No, no, no. This cannot be happening.* Kaylee braced herself and peeked into the hole.

But there was no body, muddy, bloody, partially decomposed, or otherwise.

"There's no body," she said, not bothering to temper her exasperation.

Mary stood a couple of feet behind her, clearly not eager to see for herself. But she cautiously peeked around Kaylee anyway. Mary gasped. "Is that a—" She gulped.

"Skull," George blurted, as Mrs. Banks and Chelsea rushed out of the shop. "There's a bashed skull buried facedown behind the flower shop." Only he wasn't talking to Mary. He was yelling into the phone he held with a shaky hand against his ear.

Mrs. Banks's eyes bulged. She shielded her mouth and nose with one hand and tugged Chelsea back toward the shop door.

Kaylee stared at the skull and noticed two cracks on the back of it. Who was this poor soul? And how had he or she ended up buried in the flower shop's yard?

Bear slipped out past them.

"Bear, no!" Kaylee shrieked.

He paused, his paws barely still on the edge of the pit, and gave her a questioning gaze.

"This is unacceptable," Mrs. Banks declared. "Come on Chelsea. We'll find another florist."

"No, wait." Kaylee wavered between reaching down to haul Bear away from the hole and chasing after her client—a client who could be highly influential in all the wrong ways if Kaylee didn't fix this. "This grave must be hundreds of years old, probably from the Native Americans who first inhabited the island."

Mrs. Banks sniffed in that snooty way TV shows liked to depict wealthy aristocrats, but at least she'd stopped.

Mary grabbed hold of Bear's collar, then whispered in Kaylee's ear, "The skull can't be that old or George would've discovered it when he first installed the well for your grandmother."

"You're not helping," Kaylee hissed out of the side of her mouth. To Mrs. Banks, she said, "They found skeletal remains of bison in the peat bogs and estimated that they were thousands of years old. Apparently, the peat acts like a natural embalming."

"You don't have peat here," George muttered.

Kaylee shot him a silencing glare.

"She's right, Mom," Chelsea said. "Besides, I like Kaylee's designs better than the ones we saw at that other florist. And this shop's been here for years, so you know it's not some new fly-by-night place."

"There are several quality shops on the mainland we could check out."

"The wedding is less than two months away, and it would be more hassle and expense for them to set up a wedding here than it's worth."

Mrs. Banks nudged her daughter toward the garden gate,

apparently intending to bypass going back through the store altogether. "Nothing is too much trouble for you, sweetheart."

Chelsea dug in her heels. "I think The Flower Patch will do a perfect job." She flashed Kaylee a smile that earned her an instant ten-percent discount . . . if her mother could be swayed.

Mrs. Banks shook her head. "What will people say when they find out your flowers were done by the florist with skeletons in her backyard?"

"Just remind them of all the skeletons in their closets," Mary quipped.

Chelsea giggled, but Mrs. Banks looked seriously affronted.

Kaylee swatted Mary's arm. "She's kidding. Besides, who's going to hear about it?"

The blare of a siren erupted somewhere in the distance.

Please, please, please, let it be for something else. This discovery didn't warrant the urgency of a siren. But just in case whoever took George's call didn't see it that way, Kaylee joined Mrs. Banks in prodding Chelsea toward the front gate. "I have a good idea of what you want now. How about I prepare a proposal with various options and we meet at Turtleback Country Club tomorrow afternoon to go over possible layouts? Then we can tweak it on-site to customize it to what you want."

"That sounds lovely," Chelsea said. Apparently catching on to the importance of getting her mother as far away as possible before a deputy showed up, she hurried out of the garden gate ahead of her. Chelsea held open her Bentley's passenger door for her mom, who climbed in just as a cruiser rounded the corner. "I'll text you a time," she said to Kaylee.

Kaylee backed toward the shop, waving. "Great."

Chelsea jumped in her car and sped off, and the cruiser parked in the spot she'd vacated.

Kaylee dipped her head to glance inside the police car and

waved at Deputy Dean Skenandore. As he hauled himself out of the driver's seat, she asked brightly, "How are those two adorable granddaughters of yours?" The twins had visited the island often over the summer and clearly had their grandfather wrapped around their pudgy little toddler fingers.

The deputy's usual gruff demeanor faded with his grin. "Good as gold. They're coming for another visit this weekend."

"Bear, no!" Mary's shout rose from the yard, and Kaylee raced for the gate.

Dean hurried after her. "George said he found the skull while digging up your wellhead?"

"That's right." Kaylee yanked open the gate to the side yard, grateful that the low-lying fence shielded it at least partially from the view of curious passersby. "And it has twin cracks down the back of it."

Mary held Kaylee's muddy, wriggling dachshund tight to her chest. "Bear dug up more . . . stuff. I'm going to take him inside for a bath, okay?"

"Thanks, Mary," Kaylee said. "Maybe you should stay in there and watch the shop."

Mary glanced at the hole and shuddered. "Sure thing."

"Did he unearth the rest of the body?" Deputy Skenandore asked.

"Just some clothes," George said, looking a little peaked.

Kaylee peered into the opening to see a mud-encrusted windbreaker, a metal button probably from a pair of jeans, and the rubber soles of an apparently decomposed pair of shoes.

"We're clearly not looking at an ancient burial ground," the deputy muttered.

"No," Kaylee said, "but you'd be surprised how long synthetics and metals take to decompose. I was a forensic botanist before I moved here and I saw it in several cases I worked. This body could've been here for decades."

"Not more than thirty-five years," George piped up. "That's when I installed the well for your grandmother. These days we don't bury the wellhead."

Dean nodded, then tapped something into his smartphone before circling the hole and scrutinizing the evidence from various angles. A few minutes later, his phone beeped and he glanced at the screen. "According to our forensics consultant, in these soil conditions, a body that has not been embalmed would decay within eight to twelve years." He typed in another message.

"So whoever this person was, he would've disappeared ten or more years ago." Kaylee sighed. "That leaves a twenty-five-year window."

"Yeah." The deputy tucked his phone back in his pocket. "I just asked a clerk to pull up all the unsolved missing person cases from the past thirty-five years."

"Are there that many?"

"Just the usual. Wealthy businessmen on the verge of bankruptcy or divorce. Teen runaways. An abused wife who hopefully found her way to a safer place." Dean dropped to his belly. Reaching into the hole, he pushed aside the edge of the windbreaker with the tip of his pen. A pinecone lay beneath the jacket.

"Whoa. Is that what it looks like?" Kaylee asked.

"A pinecone. Any idea how long they take to decay?" the deputy asked.

"They can take decades, thanks to the resins in them." Kaylee examined the cone more closely, mentally reviewing the evergreens known to populate the islands, and realized this wasn't one of them. "Technically, this isn't a pinecone. It's a *Picea breweriana*—Brewer's spruce. It could be a significant clue."

The deputy snorted. "Lots of people pick up pinecones and stuff them in their pockets. You should see the collections my granddaughters have, and they're toddlers."

"But the *Picea breweriana* is rare," Kaylee said. "Trust me. I spent years studying plant taxonomy. This species is only found in the Klamath Mountains of southwestern Oregon and northern California."

Dean jotted that tidbit on his notepad. "So we're looking at someone who traveled out of state."

"Or a visitor from one of those states," Kaylee said. "Assuming the cone came from the victim's pocket."

Two more deputies arrived, along with an evidence collection technician and the coroner. One of the deputies began cordoning off the shop's yard with crime scene tape.

Kaylee cringed. "Is that really necessary?" She gave Dean her best pleading face. She'd already almost lost Mrs. Banks's business this morning. If the woman saw crime scene tape on her next visit, that would seal the order's doom—and likely the doom of every order from any other country club member with a daughter getting married in the next twelve months, if Mrs. Banks had any say in the matter. And Kaylee had a bad feeling Mrs. Banks would ensure everyone knew her thoughts on The Flower Patch. Kaylee stifled a groan.

Dean took pity on her and instructed the deputy to string the tape on the inside of the fence, where it wouldn't be so visible from the street. "And turn off your cruiser's lights," he barked. "We don't want to attract the whole neighborhood."

But it was too late. People were already heading their way up the street.

Dean asked George a slew of questions and meticulously recorded the answers on his notepad. "Okay, George, you're free to go. It'll likely be a few days before we release the scene."

"What?" Kaylee's voice hit a new octave. "You mean he can't fix my well before he goes? I don't have any water. And I have hundreds of thirsty plants inside."

"Isn't Mrs. Roberts a friend of yours?" the deputy asked.

"Yes, but—" Kaylee furrowed her brow, not following what that had to do with anything.

"Why don't you just run next door to her shop to fill your watering jugs?"

The man clearly has no idea how many trips that would take, nor does he seem to care that I can only do it after hours or when Mary can watch the shop. Realizing it wasn't a battle she'd win, however, Kaylee shrugged. "I guess we will make do. May I get back to work inside now?"

"Sure. Go ahead. I know where to find you if I have any questions."

Kaylee was about to slip in the side door when she spotted her friend Jessica Roberts hurrying over from her bakery, Death by Chocolate, which was right next door. Kaylee let herself out the gate to meet her.

Jessica rushed up and clasped Kaylee's forearms in a stranglehold. "Is it true?"

"Is what true?"

"One of my customers said there's a dead body in your backyard."

Kaylee shushed her and glanced over at the crowd gathered on the sidewalk, straining to see what was happening on the other side of the fence. Desperate to get away from prying eyes and ears, Kaylee ushered Jessica into the shop to fill her in on the morning's developments.

"I just knew something bad was going to happen today," Jessica said as they ducked inside. "Oliver has been drooping all morning."

Oliver was Jessica's prized lavender geranium, and Jessica also believed him to be the predictor of all things unpleasant about to befall herself or her nearest and dearest. He had a spot of honor on the counter in Death by Chocolate.

Before Kaylee had a chance to give Jessica the lowdown, their friend DeeDee Wilcox, owner of the mystery bookstore down the street, rushed in too. At the sight of Kaylee, DeeDee splayed her hand against her chest. "Thank goodness you're okay! As soon as I saw all the cruisers pull up in front of your shop, I booted out my customers and closed my place so I could make sure nothing had happened to you."

"I'm fine," Kaylee said. "Although I'm not sure I'll be able to say the same for my business." She peeked out the window at the growing crowd. "This isn't the kind of word-of-mouth publicity a florist hopes for." She explained what had transpired that morning.

"Oh wow," DeeDee said, following her gaze out the window. "But hey, you never know. The notoriety could bring in more clients."

"And here comes a couple up the walk now," Mary said cheerily from the front of the store where she was working on the window display.

"Oh no." Kaylee vainly attempted to prop up the droopiest plants. "I still haven't watered."

Jessica squeezed her arm. "We can help with that. DeeDee and I will go fill some water jugs for you right now. Don't worry. I'm sure the deputies will clear out before you know it."

"Thanks. You guys are the best."

"Don't mention it," DeeDee said as she and Jessica headed out the door.

"Uh-oh." Mary stared out the front window. "That couple must've changed their mind. I don't see them now." Mary craned her neck and peered in the direction of the crowd gawking at the goings-on in the side yard. "That's a lot of people. We should put out a sale sign."

Kaylee shook her head. "I don't want to capitalize on this.

That's someone's missing loved one back there. A family somewhere has been wondering what happened to that person for years, and now they're going to find out the worst news possible."

Mary sobered. "You're right. If you think about it, at least one good thing should come of your water problem."

"How do you figure?"

"It'll finally bring closure for the victim's family."

Kaylee sighed. "If the sheriff's department can ID him or her."

"Oh wow." Mary was back to peering out the window. "Even Mr. Phelps is out there. I didn't think he ever got out anymore."

"The owner of the computer store?" Kaylee snuck a peek out the side window.

"His son runs the store these days."

"I don't think I've seen him out in daylight before."

Mary nodded. "Just goes to show you how powerful morbid curiosity is."

The bell above the shop's front door tinkled and a handsome couple, who appeared to be in their early fifties, strolled in.

Bear let out a friendly woof and meandered over to give them a sniff. The woman stooped down and held her hand out for him to sniff, then stroked the soft fur on his head, which was still a little damp from the bath Mary had given him.

"What a cutie you are," she cooed.

"Good morning," Kaylee said. "How may I help you?"

The gentleman flashed her a warm smile. "Is Bea around?"

"No, I'm sorry. She's moved to Arizona. I'm her granddaughter Kaylee."

The man reached for Kaylee's hand and enveloped it between his. "Pleased to meet you."

Kaylee glanced down, surprised by how warm his hands were.

"I was just reminiscing with Raylene," he went on, releasing Kaylee's hand and surveying the shop. "I was telling her how my first job was here. I made deliveries on my bicycle, watered plants, that sort of thing."

"Oh, Grandma will be sorry she missed you, Mr. . . . ?"

The man gave Kaylee a bemused look, clearly thinking she should know who he was.

She took in his mildly-salted dark hair and the fine lines that framed his eyes and creased his forehead. His broad, muscular torso said he took his fitness seriously. His left ring finger was void of a ring as was the woman's. But nothing about his appearance rang a bell.

Mary joined them and extended her hand to the man. "Congressman, so nice of you to drop in." To Kaylee she added, "Congressman Munk grew up on the island. Now he just visits the old family home in the summers, I believe."

The man nodded. "Call me Ted."

"You'll have to forgive Kaylee," Mary said. "She doesn't pay much attention to politics."

His smile broadened. "Well, we'll have to remedy that. Won't we, Raylene?" He glanced at the slender redhead accompanying him. "After all, the election is in two months."

Raylene pulled a button from her handbag and handed it to Kaylee.

"Oh." The button said *Ted Munk for Governor* in red and blue. "Um, thank you."

"You are registered to vote, aren't you?" Ted asked.

"Yes, of course."

Ted's rather contagious smile spread across his face once more. "Well, if you have any concerns or questions at all, don't hesitate to call." He passed her his business card, but held it a tad longer than necessary after she accepted it. His eyes twinkled. "I'm here to serve," he said. "The citizens of Turtle Cove hold an extra-special place in my heart."

"We appreciate that," Mary said. "I was thinking that if our citizens spotted the future governor leaving The Flower Patch with a lovely floral bouquet, it would go a long way to mitigating the effect the scene outside is having on Kaylee's business."

"Mary!" Kaylee gasped.

"No." Ted held up his hand. "She's absolutely right. I'll take two mixed floral arrangements in those plastic vases I can poke into the ground. They're for my parents' graves."

Kaylee nodded solemnly and set to work.

Ted meandered over to the counter and watched. "Have any of the deputies spoken to you? Do they know who the victim is?"

"Not that I've heard yet." Kaylee shoved the image of the dirt-encrusted skull from her mind as she poked a mix of *Zantedeschia aethiopica, Gerbera jamesonii, Dahlia pinnata, Iris germanica,* and *Trientalis borealis*—or as in layman's terms, ivory calla lilies, red gerbera daisies, yellow dahlias, blue irises, and starflowers—into a memorial vase. She finished it off with greenery, then presented it for Ted's inspection. "How's this?"

"Perfect. If I win the governor's race, I might just have to put you on retainer for all our events."

Kaylee blushed. Considering the governor's mansion was in Olympia, over 150 miles away, she didn't have any illusions he was serious. Still, it was nice of him to say.

She quickly made up the second vase, and his assistant paid for them.

"Don't worry," Ted said as he reached the door. "I'll speak to the sheriff. See about getting you your yard back as expeditiously as possible."

"I'd appreciate that. Thank you."

He graced her with another of his warm smiles, nodded to Mary, then trailed his assistant outside.

As soon as the door closed behind him, Mary rolled her eyes. "He hasn't changed a bit."

"How do you mean?"

"He's obsessed with winning whatever he puts his mind to. He's been that way ever since he beat my kid sister in their fifth-grade spelling bee."

Kaylee picked up the button Ted's assistant had given her and chucked it in the closest drawer. "I suppose a politician has to court votes wherever he goes."

Mary laughed. "I'm pretty sure he's interested in courting more than your vote."

2

"Proprietor Kaylee Bleu is digging up more than flowers at The Flower Patch in Turtle Cove," the radio announcer said in a tone straight out of *The Twilight Zone.*

Kaylee snapped off her car's radio as she parked in front of her shop. "I wasn't even the one digging," she grumbled to Bear as she grabbed her ringing cell phone.

"Hey, Miss Bleu." Chelsea's bubbly voice rang over the line. "I think we should postpone our meeting."

Kaylee's heart plummeted. She needed this job. She doubted her grandmother's cash flow had ever been this tight at the end of a busy tourist season. "Is your mom still uncomfortable about the investigation?"

Chelsea snorted as if that was the understatement of the year. "Yeah, she's in a total snit over the radio report."

Kaylee muffled a groan.

"I suggested we spend the day shopping on the mainland for bridesmaids' gifts. Hopefully by tomorrow the talk will have died down."

Fat chance of that on an island this size. Not when the birth of twin foals at the Pomeroys' horse farm was the lead story the same day an earthquake hit Vancouver Island, less than fifty miles west of them. With Kaylee's luck, Orcas Island's weekly newspaper would put out a special edition just to cover the story while it was still hot. "Could we make it Monday instead?" Kaylee asked. "I'm helping out with our church's youth group tomorrow afternoon."

"Even better."

"Great. I'll see you then."

Kaylee pushed open her SUV's driver's side door and watched as a car crawled along the street in her direction, then parked in front of Death by Chocolate. The delicious smell of baked pastries and chocolate emanating from Jessica's shop almost tempted Kaylee to take a few extra minutes to indulge in coffee and a muffin—and maybe a little self-pity—before lugging in the jugs of water she'd brought from home. But the sight of a couple pausing at the bakery's door and looking her way, or more precisely toward the crime scene tape still gracing the side yard, changed her mind.

Bear, still sitting in the car, gave a sharp bark.

"Yeah, my sentiments exactly." Kaylee adjusted his red-striped bow tie and let him out. "I think I'd rather get straight to work than field questions about the body in the backyard from Jessica's customers." She popped her trunk and hefted out two of the three-gallon jugs she'd filled. Bear dashed to the front door. He stood up against it and it swung open.

Kaylee froze, six feet from the door, and glanced up and down the street. "Mary isn't here yet." Wariness tingled down her spine. "I was pretty distracted last night," she muttered to herself. "I guess I could've forgotten to lock the door." She stared at Bear sitting in the open doorway, his tongue lolling out. *And forgotten to latch it properly so even a twenty-pound dachshund could push it open?*

She set down the jugs and cautiously peeked inside. "Hello?" she called out in as cheerful a voice as she could muster. "Anyone here?"

No one answered. The showroom appeared in perfect order.

Leaving the front door ajar, she walked to the back of the three-story Victorian mansion and glanced in the other rooms. At the foot of the stairs, she cocked her ear toward the second floor.

Not a sound.

"Hello? Anyone upstairs?"

Bear bounded up the steps, and Kaylee followed him to the second-story landing, then from room to room. The floor was deserted, so they headed up to the third story. Bear's little feet scurried across the old pine floors, but there was no other sound.

Finally, Bear let out a happy bark, circled Kaylee's legs twice, and then headed down to the main floor.

"I guess we're good." She went back outside and retrieved the water jugs from the walkway.

The instant she returned, Bear started barking somewhere at the back of the building.

Kaylee grabbed one of the white birch branches she had for sale near the front of the store and held it like a baseball bat. "Who's there?"

Bear's barking came in sporadic bursts, as if he were snapping at something.

Maybe a bird or a squirrel or something had made its way in. No matter how much she tried, some creature always seemed to find another way to sneak into the old place.

Kaylee edged down the hallway, just as Bear backed out of the bathroom, barking at whoever, or whatever, he'd cornered inside. Kaylee peeked around the door's edge. At the sight of a snake dropping through the cracked window, she let out a glass-rattling scream and leaped back.

She blinked rapidly, then realized . . . "That's not a snake!" Kaylee stomped into the room, closed the toilet lid and stepped up on it. She grabbed hold of the dangling water hose, then stood on her tiptoes and peered out the high window. The hose was coupled to the outside tap on Jessica's shop, but whoever fished it through the window had disappeared.

"Hello?" Kaylee called again.

"Hello," said a deep voice from behind her.

Startled, she toppled sideways.

Reese Holt lunged forward and caught her. He helped her land almost gracefully. "Sorry. I didn't mean to scare you. Jess said you needed water."

"I thought the hose was a snake." Kaylee gulped a deep breath, and with it, his outdoorsy pine scent.

Reese wore his usual worn jeans, work boots, and plaid shirt. He flashed her his disarming smile.

She shouldn't be surprised he'd have a solution to her water problem. The carpenter had been a trusted friend and big help to her grandmother, and he had transferred those qualities to his friendship with Kaylee. She tipped back her head to meet his eyes. They always reminded her of the color of the sky just before sunset.

Kaylee mentally shook herself. She had more pressing matters than the color of Reese's eyes to deal with at the moment.

Releasing her arm, he took the hose from her, dragged more in, and then laid the end in the bathtub where a leak wouldn't do any damage. "There. That should help you handle the essentials until your well is recommissioned."

"That's fabulous. Thanks so much for doing this."

"No problem." Reese's long stride ate up the short distance to the front of the store. "Anything else you need a hand with while I'm here?"

Clearly disappointed that the excitement was over, Bear flopped onto his bed by the cash register.

"Not unless you have any idea who was buried in my yard and how he got there," she said. "Being a crime scene isn't exactly good for business."

"Jessica said the disappearance probably happened when she was a teenager, or maybe in her early twenties?"

Kaylee did some quick math. "Yeah, that sounds about right."

"So I would've been in elementary school." Reese scratched his whiskers, his gaze drifting to the front window. "The only big thing I remember happening then was a teenage girl getting killed in a hit-and-run boating accident."

"They never found the body?"

"They did. But . . ." His eyes lit with a new thought. "I think the teenage boy they suspected of the crime disappeared not long afterward."

Kaylee gasped in horror at the possibility the remains belonged to the suspected teen. At the same time, a morbid hope swelled her chest. If the crushed skull did belong to the missing boy, the sheriff's department would be that much closer to being done with her yard.

"You could check the newspaper archives at the library," Reese said.

The bells above the front door announced Mary's arrival.

"Or Mary might remember his name." Reese repeated the story to her.

"Sure. I remember that. I can't believe I didn't think of it yesterday. The boy's name was Danny Lane. His mom had run off with another man when the boy was really young. And his dad was no prize. It really was no wonder he started running wild."

Through the front window, Kaylee saw Sheriff Eddie Maddox's car pull to the curb, and she rushed outside. "Sheriff, I'm so glad you're here. We think we've figured out the victim."

"Danny Lane," he said.

Kaylee's lungs deflated. "Yes." She should've known he'd have deduced as much when he reviewed the department's list of missing persons.

"The coroner confirmed the ID twenty minutes ago by matching the skull's teeth to the boy's dental records."

"Do you think someone murdered him to avenge the girl he killed in the boating accident?" Kaylee asked.

Sheriff Maddox's cheek muscle twitched. "The coroner hasn't found any evidence of foul play."

Kaylee shot him a baffled look. "What about the fractures in the back of his skull?"

"It's consistent with a tumble into an open pit and knocking his head on the wellhead."

"Except that George said he was facedown."

"Because he likely managed to roll over in an attempt to crawl out, but inadvertently brought a landslide of dirt over himself, which prevented George from spotting him before he filled the hole the next day."

Kaylee frowned. To get the twin fracture lines she'd seen, Danny's head would've had to have struck the edge of the wellhead at least twice.

Sheriff Maddox tilted his head. "You'll have your yard back soon. I thought you'd be happy."

Kaylee couldn't explain it, but the sheriff's theory didn't sit right with her. "What was Danny doing in the shop's yard?"

"I'll tell you what he was doing," growled a voice like gravel.

Startled, Kaylee whirled around to find Glen Phelps, the elderly electronics storeowner she'd hardly seen since she moved to Turtle Cove.

"He was a troublemaker." Glen punctuated the statement with a rap of his cane on the sidewalk, then let out a raspy cough. "He'd graffiti our store walls, soap the windows, pilfer product. He was probably prowling around the yard trying to find a way in and mess up her flowers somehow. He'd had run-ins with her before."

"He had a history of misdemeanors," Sheriff Maddox said. "The old-timers I questioned also believed the boy's disappearance confirmed everyone's suspicions that he was responsible for the boating accident that killed Joelle Spiece the week before your well was dug."

"But clearly Danny didn't flee to escape conviction like they must've assumed," Kaylee said. "So what does that tell you?"

"If you ask me, he got what he deserved." Mr. Phelps leaned heavily on his cane. "You sneak around where you shouldn't, you pay."

The sheriff crossed his arms. "How about you both go about your business and leave the investigation to the professionals? I'll be in touch." He climbed back into his car and drove away.

With a harrumph, Glen turned on his heel and walked in the direction of his store. Kaylee approached The Flower Patch's front door just as Reese came out carrying a bouquet.

"Giving us business *and* ensuring our plants are watered?" Kaylee smiled. "You're a gem."

His responding smile was a shade sheepish. "Congressman Munk called in the bouquet order. I told Mary I could deliver it since I'm headed to his estate to start building him a new deck."

"Ah well, thank you for that."

"What did Maddox have to say?"

"Our victim was, in fact, Danny Lane. They think his death was an accident. He had a reputation for vandalizing the local businesses."

Reese studied her for a long moment. "But you have your doubts?"

"Yeah."

He raised an eyebrow at her. "It's not your problem. Our sheriff's department is more than capable of handling it."

Kaylee shrugged.

"If I can help you with anything else, don't hesitate to call, okay?"

"Like I said—you're a gem." A moment after he headed for his truck, Kaylee remembered the unlatched shop door. "Hey, how'd you get in my shop this morning?"

"The front door was unlocked."

3

"Someone's sweet on you," Mary said in a singsong voice as Kaylee stepped back into the shop.

Kaylee glanced out the front window at Reese's truck pulling away from the curb, and her heart quickened a little. "You think so?"

"The only other customers who have bought three arrangements in two days are brides."

"Huh?" Kaylee's attention snapped back to Mary. "Oh, you mean Congressman Munk."

"That's Ted to you." Mary grinned. "He specifically asked if you made your own deliveries and I said sometimes. But Reese overheard Ted on the line and insisted I make up the bouquet while he waited to save you the trip."

"Sounds to me like Reese is the one sweet on Kaylee," said a little gray-haired lady who shuffled out from behind the shelves of new-baby gifts. Kaylee recognized her as Marianne Crosby, one of her grandmother's regular customers, whose granddaughter was expecting in October.

Mary rolled her eyes at Marianne. "Reese hasn't dated since his fiancée took off to 'find herself.'"

Marianne shrugged. "For someone not shopping for flowers, he hangs around here a lot. Don't you think?"

"He was here just as often to help Bea," Mary said. "I hope you're not about to suggest he was sweet on her. He heard we had some trouble, and he wanted to help. He's a nice guy."

"I won't argue with that." Marianne picked up a small succulent planter with a balloon tucked inside that said *Welcome,*

Baby! and brought it to the cash register. "He'll make some lucky girl a fine husband one day."

Kaylee thought Marianne was starting to sound like her grandmother. Bea just couldn't understand how Kaylee could be forty and still single. Never mind all she'd managed to accomplish in that time—a PhD in plant taxonomy, being a professor at the university, consulting with local law enforcement in Seattle and now on Orcas Island as a forensic botanist.

After Marianne left, Kaylee filled Mary in on her talk with Sheriff Maddox.

Mary listened, then nodded. "I seem to recall that the coincidental timing of Danny's disappearance was what clinched the old sheriff's theory that Danny caused Joelle's boat to capsize."

"Sure," Kaylee said, "but now that it's clear Danny didn't run, Sheriff Maddox doesn't seem to be questioning the theory. Or entertaining the possibility that his death wasn't an accident."

"I'm not surprised," Mary said. "Maddox has enough open investigations to keep him working late into the night without fabricating a thirty-five-year-old murder where there wasn't one."

"But what if there was?"

Mary dipped her head and peered over her glasses at Kaylee. "It would be better for the shop if you let it go."

Kaylee sighed. She knew that was true, but for some reason, she just couldn't. What if that poor boy had been murdered, but no one was willing to dig into it because he had supposedly caused another teen's death? He deserved justice too.

"Reese sure was a lifesaver hooking up that hose," Mary said, pulling Kaylee from her thoughts. "I noticed the shipment of potted flowers that came in a couple of days ago isn't looking so good. Would you mind watering them while I finish up this arrangement?"

Kaylee smacked herself on the forehead. "Oh wow, with everything going on, I totally forgot to check those over. I'll do it now."

Kaylee filled her watering can from the hose Reese fished through the bathroom window and carried it over to the pots of blue *Hydrangea macrophylla* clustered below a sunny window in the back room. "You are pretty droopy, aren't you?" she said to the plant closest to her as she plucked a few dried flowers from its stems. She pulled the paper wrapping down from around the pot and raked her fingers over the soil to fluff it up. "Ew," she squealed at the slimy feeling of a slug against her finger. She parted the leaves and reached in to pull it out.

A head popped out of the soil. And it didn't belong to a slug.

She screamed and snapped her hand back.

Mary raced into the room. "What's wrong?"

"There's a snake in the pot!"

Mary relaxed and actually had the nerve to chuckle. "You do know there are no poisonous snakes on Orcas Island."

"Sure, but it's buried in a pot that came from the mainland."

"Good point." Mary grabbed the steel garbage can from beside the back door, dumped the plant cuttings and such into a nearby empty box, then flipped it upside down over the plant pot. "That should keep it contained until animal control gets here."

Kaylee called animal control and they arrived in less than twenty minutes. While the two workers sealed it, pot and all, in their own container, Kaylee called her supplier on the mainland to find out where the plant had originated.

"The plant came from Florida," she informed the animal control workers.

"Good thing the snake didn't bite you," one said. "From the glimpse I got of it, it could be a copperhead. We'll figure it out and let you know."

Kaylee handed them the phone number and address of her supplier so they could document how it arrived on the island.

Mary, standing in the room's doorway, her hand splayed protectively at her throat, asked, "Did you check the other pots to make sure there aren't more?"

The second animal control officer nodded. "The rest are clear."

Mary and Kaylee sighed together in relief. Kaylee walked the officers and their cargo to their truck. At the curious looks of passersby, she was happy Mrs. Banks, at least, was off the island today. Returning to the shop, Kaylee shuddered at the thought of the snake slithering across a customer's path. Her newest competition wouldn't have to undercut her prices—everyone would flock there for safety.

"Why don't you go next door and get yourself a coffee?" Mary suggested in a motherly tone. "I can watch the shop."

"Are you sure you don't mind?"

She made a sweeping motion with her hands. "Go on."

Bear whined.

Kaylee turned to him. "No boy, you stay here with Mary. I won't be long."

He plopped on his behind and gave her his saddest face.

"That won't work. You know dogs aren't allowed in Jess's bakery, silly." Kaylee reached for the door handle, and remembered about it being unlocked that morning. "Have you noticed anything missing or out of place around here?"

Mary glanced around the showroom. "No, why?"

"It seems I forgot to lock the front door when I left last night."

"Oh!" Mary opened the cash register, lifted the front tray, and counted the larger bills sitting beneath it. "The money seems to be all here."

"We've got that going for us, at least."

With a wave, Kaylee left and headed to Jessica's bakery next door.

The aroma of brewing coffee and fresh-baked goodies—chocolate brownies, apple and cinnamon pies, breads that made Kaylee's mouth water—soothed her frayed nerves.

Most of the tables were occupied. DeeDee sat at a table near the back with Lydia Mack, one of her bookstore's best customers, and they motioned for her to join them.

As Kaylee headed their way, Jessica hurried over too. "How's the hose working?"

"It's great. Thanks so much for asking Reese to run it." Kaylee slipped into the chair opposite Lydia.

"It wasn't my idea," Jessica said. "He came by first thing this morning and asked if he could hook up to my outside tap."

Kaylee's mood lifted at that bit of news. Reese really was a thoughtful guy.

"What was the animal control van doing at your shop?" Jessica asked, souring Kaylee's mood again.

Kaylee involuntarily shuddered at the memory of trying to pluck the potentially venomous snake from the pot. "There was a snake in one of my potted plants."

"Do you think that new florist in Eastsound snuck it into the shop to try to scare your customers her way?" Jessica asked. She tended to think there was a conspiracy behind just about everything.

"What a dirty trick," Lydia said.

Kaylee shook her head. "It came in with a plant recently shipped from Florida." She left out that it might have been a copperhead. That was a rumor she didn't need getting around. She'd already lost enough wedding business to the island's newest flower shop.

"I wouldn't put it past that new florist," DeeDee said. "I hate to tell you this, but a brutal review of The Flower Patch popped up online a couple of days ago, and I'm pretty sure she was behind it."

"Why didn't you tell me?"

"You had enough to worry about, and I wanted to see if I could prove my theory first."

"Did you?" Jessica asked.

"Sort of," DeeDee said. "I traced the reviewer's handle to Northern California."

Jessica's eyebrows shot up. "That's where the new florist is from."

DeeDee nodded. "Exactly. My guess is, she got one of her friends or relatives to trash The Flower Patch to drag down its rating."

Kaylee sighed. "Or it could've been a tourist who wasn't happy with the service he received."

DeeDee shook her head. "Trust me. Nothing this reviewer said rang true."

Not that a casual reader would know it. Kaylee muffled another sigh.

"I'm sorry," DeeDee said. "I didn't mean to add to your frustrations." She leaned across the table. "So what's the scoop on the body?" As owner of the town's mystery bookshop, she was always reading them—and she was just as eager to delve into real-life mysteries too.

Lydia murmured her eagerness to know as well.

Kaylee repeated what she'd learned from the sheriff.

"There would've been plenty of people with motive to murder Joelle's suspected killer," Lydia said. In her midsixties, she was old enough to remember. "Her father was beside himself with grief. That girl was the apple of his eye."

"It sounds as if a few shopkeepers had motive too," DeeDee added, even though she was too young to know from firsthand experience.

"Because of the vandalism Danny had a reputation for, you mean?" Jessica asked.

DeeDee pinched off a bite of chocolate croissant and popped it into her mouth. "That, and I overheard Glen Phelps and the butcher reminiscing outside his shop on my way here. They clearly had no sympathy for the boy."

Kaylee's stomach grumbled. "Did Danny's father ever take him on vacation off the island?" She turned to Lydia. "Do you know?"

Lydia shook her head. "Not likely. He was too cheap. Why?"

"A rare variety of spruce cone was found with Danny's jacket."

"Good to see you, Congressman," said a deep voice behind Kaylee.

Kaylee glanced over her shoulder, surprised she hadn't heard Ted come in. He and his assistant sat at the booth directly behind hers. Ted had his back to Kaylee and was talking animatedly to a man standing beside their table, but Raylene made eye contact and nodded a greeting. Kaylee waited a couple of seconds, expecting Raylene to point out her presence to Ted. When she didn't, Kaylee opted not to interrupt their powwow.

Since they'd only met once, it was hardly surprising Ted hadn't recognized her by the back of her head. And if they were in the middle of a power meeting or a date, it was understandable Raylene wouldn't mention Kaylee to him. Or maybe she'd assumed Kaylee would say something. Should she have?

Second-guessing her decision to not say hello, Kaylee gnawed on her bottom lip. Ted had just placed an order at her shop, after all. She paused at that thought. If Ted had been headed into town, why did he ask Mary if Kaylee could deliver the bouquet to his house? Was the order merely a pretense to see her again?

Kaylee shook her head at the ridiculous notion. If that were true, he'd be sharing coffee with her, not Raylene.

"I remember Joelle's boyfriend being pretty irate over the sheriff letting Danny get away," Lydia said, drawing Kaylee's attention back to their conversation.

"Do you remember his name?" Kaylee asked.

"Sure. It's Digger. Neil 'Digger' Dykstra. He owns a big landscaping company."

"He was out watching the deputies inspect your yard yesterday," DeeDee said. "I saw him when I walked by."

"Everyone and their grandmother watched." Jessica rolled her eyes. "Then stopped in here hoping to get some juicy gossip."

Kaylee's chest tightened. Her wedding order with Chelsea Banks was already hanging by a thread. And based on Mrs. Banks's reaction to the shop's so-called scandal, Kaylee could count on losing business from other country club members who shared the woman's skewed sense of propriety. Kaylee pressed her fingers to her throbbing temples.

"Can I get you a coffee?" Jessica motioned to her waitress, who immediately hurried over with a cup.

"Thank you." Kaylee took a sip. Maybe Mary was right. Maybe she should just accept whatever verdict Eddie settled on and let the rumormongering die a natural death.

But her stomach churned at the memory of Danny's fractured skull. She set down her coffee mug. "I can't shake this feeling that Danny was murdered."

Everyone around the table nodded. "The whole island mourned that poor girl's death," Lydia said. "Once word got out that Danny was the chief suspect, it wouldn't surprise me if some vigilante decided to take the law into his own hands."

"But the sheriff assumed Danny fled." Kaylee studied her coffee mug. "So wasn't everyone still fuming when they failed to capture him?"

"They sure were." Kathy Fitz, the town's head librarian, stood at their table.

"Hi, Kathy," Kaylee said. "Do you know something we don't?"

"As soon as I heard the news story on the radio this morning,

I checked the newspaper archives," Kathy said. "For months after the accident, there were letters to the editor, complaining about how little the sheriff seemed to be doing to find Danny."

"Any from the shopkeepers around town?" Kaylee asked.

"No. They were probably just happy the vandalism had finally stopped."

Or happy they'd put a stop to it. "What about from Joelle's father? Or Neil Dykstra, her boyfriend?"

"No. I doubt they were in any kind of state to write letters," Kathy said.

Kaylee nodded and made a mental note to ask Mary if she could find out from her former law enforcement connections if the men had continued to press the sheriff personally. If they hadn't, it could have been because they'd known Danny was dead.

DeeDee articulated what Kaylee was thinking. "If we can figure out who stopped being upset about the sheriff department's lack of results after Danny's disappearance, we'll have his killer?"

Kaylee shrugged. "Maybe."

"What else are you thinking?" Jessica asked.

Kaylee finished her coffee and let out a ragged sigh. "That between Danny's dysfunctional family and his petty crimes, he was an easy scapegoat for Joelle's death."

DeeDee raised her eyebrows. "You don't think he did it?"

"I don't know what to think. If Danny fell to his death while prowling about my shop's yard in the dark, then the fact he 'disappeared'"—Kaylee punctuated the word with air quotes—"had nothing to do with a guilty conscience or fear of getting caught."

"Yeah, it kind of makes the vigilante theory more believable," DeeDee said.

"Did the sheriff's department have any proof Danny rammed Joelle's boat?" Kaylee asked Kathy and Lydia.

Kathy nodded. "A witness claimed to have seen Danny sneaking around the marina that night."

Jessica slapped the table, her eyes glowing with the light they got when her mind had cooked up a new conspiracy theory. "Maybe Danny was killed to shift suspicion away from Joelle's *real* murderer."

4

Kaylee had never been so relieved to see closing time roll around. Since she'd returned from Death by Chocolate, the only people who had graced her shop's doorstep had been reporters. She had no idea where they'd all come from. Of course it hadn't helped that the sheriff's department still had her side yard cordoned off.

Bear whined at her as she stood in the bathroom doorway debating whether to fish the gardening hose back out of the window so she could secure it.

"It's pretty high up. What do you think?" she asked him, not really expecting an answer.

He lay down as if settling in for a wait.

"You're right. Better safe than sorry." She tipped the hose out the window, then fastened the latch and checked it twice. She checked the back door and ground floor windows, then locked the front door behind her and tested it. "We're going to do some visiting. How does that sound?" Kaylee asked Bear, as she let him into the car.

He clambered into the front seat and let out an approving woof.

"You need to be on your best behavior." She glanced at the address she'd gotten from the Internet for Walter Spiece, Joelle Spiece's father. "This man has to be in his seventies, maybe even his eighties, and might not appreciate rambunctiousness, okay?"

Bear ignored her as he watched the scenery whiz by.

Walter Spiece's cedar-shake house sat on the edge of town. The lawn was neatly trimmed, and a cute little flower bed hugged the front porch.

"Well, if his yard is anything to go by, he must still be fairly active." Kaylee glanced at the clock on her dash. "Hopefully we won't be bothering him during dinner." She parked in the driveway and hesitated a moment before turning off the ignition. Maybe she should've gone home first and had supper herself. Then again, if she left it too late, she might interrupt his favorite evening game show. Kaylee's dad hated being disturbed in the middle of *Jeopardy*. Maybe Joelle's dad was the same way.

Bear scratched at the car door.

"You're right. We're here now. Let's do this." Her stomach somersaulted. What if the man didn't appreciate her stirring up memories of his daughter's death? According to Mary, his wife had died years ago and his other daughter lived off the island, so Kaylee hoped he'd just enjoy having company for a while.

Bear raced to the front door.

"Best behavior," Kaylee reminded him as she knocked.

Bear sat on his rump and eagerly stared at the door.

A few moments passed and Kaylee knocked again. Louder.

A stooped, white-haired man opened the door. "Sorry, I don't move as quickly as I used to." His gaze fell to Bear and a grin broke out on his face. "What a handsome fella you are." He stretched out his hand, then slowly bent lower so the short-legged dachshund could reach.

Bear gave the man's fingers an exuberant lick, tail whipping from side to side.

He laughed. "I used to have a dog just like you when I was a boy. His name was Peanut."

"This is Bear," Kaylee said. "I'm Kaylee Bleu. I took over ownership of The Flower Patch from my grandmother a while ago." She mentally kicked herself for not thinking to bring him a nice bouquet for his home.

"I don't have much cause to buy flowers these days," he

said, straightening with some effort. "The wife's been gone for fifteen years."

"Oh, I'm not trying to sell anything, Mr. Spiece. You might've heard on the radio that human remains were discovered in my shop's yard."

A car rumbled by on the street, muffling her explanation.

Mr. Spiece stepped back from the door. "Come in. I can't hear you with the traffic and I can't stand too long these days. Would you like some tea?"

"I'm fine. Thank you."

He motioned her into a quaint living room and picking up the TV remote, flicked it off. He sat in a well-used recliner and gestured to the sofa opposite him. "Have a seat, young lady. C'mon, Bear. You can sit with me." He patted his knees.

Bear lifted his front paws as high on the man's legs as he could reach and Mr. Spiece boosted him the rest of the way.

Kaylee circled the room admiring the family photos lining the shelves before settling onto the sofa. "You have a lovely home and yard."

Preoccupied by lavishing attention on Bear, Mr. Spiece responded without glancing her way. "Can't take credit for that, I'm afraid. Digger keeps the yard in tip-top shape and I have a housekeeper come in once a week."

"Digger Dykstra?" Kaylee asked. "I thought he was more of a landscaper than yard maintenance man."

"Yup. He's the best landscaper on the island. But he's like family. Dated my Joelle for four years before she died, and insists on doing what needs to be done."

"He sounds very kind."

"He's a good man."

"Is that him in the vacation picture?" She pointed to an aged picture on the bookshelf of the family with mountains in the background. Walter, his wife, and two girls beamed at the camera, along with two well-groomed young men who flanked the girls.

Walter looked up at the picture and his eyes misted over. "The lad on the left."

"Was this taken in the Klamath Mountains?"

Walter frowned. "I can't remember." His forehead wrinkled as if that fact deeply disturbed him. "It was taken the last family vacation we went on before we lost Joelle." He shook his head and returned his attention to Bear. "I should remember."

"I'm very sorry for your loss." Kaylee had been about to say that knowing the location wasn't important, except that it was—or, at least, it could be. One of the people in that picture could have come home with a Brewer's spruce cone in his pocket, and then lost it at an inopportune time.

Mr. Spiece nodded, his attention fixed on Bear. "Jo-Jo always loved going out on the boat. She was so proud of Digger's racing skills." He shook his head. "Funny how we never worried about her out on the water. Girls just weren't reckless like the boys could be. So we never thought . . ." His gaze drifted to the family pictures. "Neil has never forgiven himself for working late that night and letting Joelle take the boat out alone. He never moved on."

"'If only' is hard to live with," Kaylee said softly.

Mr. Spiece swiped at his damp eyes.

Kaylee regarded him with sympathy. "I imagine it's hard with the discovery of Danny Lane's remains stirring up questions once again."

"What are you talking about?"

"Hasn't the sheriff talked to you?"

"No," he said sharply.

Kaylee bit her lip, debating how much more to say. He clearly hadn't heard her explanation at the door. But she'd already let the cat out of the bag, so to speak, so she might as well see where it led. "They identified remains found in my shop's yard as Danny Lane's."

He squinted at her. "What are you getting at?"

Bear jumped from his lap, probably unnerved by the man's sharp tone.

Kaylee's pulse quickened. Shock could've triggered the man's anger. But what if it was a guilty conscience? After all, no one would've had stronger motive to murder the supposed killer of his daughter. "I truly didn't mean to upset you. I thought knowing where the boy is after all these years might give you some closure."

Mr. Spiece pushed to his feet. "Nothing can bring back my Joelle."

"No, of course not." Not wanting to overstay her welcome, Kaylee stood too. "Before moving here, I consulted law enforcement as a forensic botanist in cases like this, and families seemed to find some comfort in knowing justice was served. I hope you can too."

He shuffled toward the front door.

Kaylee dutifully followed, but some inner compulsion wouldn't let her leave without pressing him a little harder for answers. "Or are you afraid Danny might not have been responsible for your daughter's death after all?"

Mr. Spiece's attention snapped back to hers, his face pasty. "Why would you say that?"

"Since Danny didn't run away as the investigators had assumed. As I understand, his disappearance was what clinched his guilt for most people."

The man began to tremble.

Now she felt like dirt. "I'm sorry. Let me help you to your chair." She reached for his arm, but he swatted her away.

"Just go. I want to be left alone."

Kaylee scooped up Bear, but then wavered, unwilling to leave the frail man in such distress. "Will you be all right? I could make you tea before I go. Get you a glass of water?"

Bear strained toward Mr. Spiece and licked the man's hands.

A smidgen of color returned to his cheeks, and a whisper of a smile played on his lips as he scratched behind the dog's ears. "You're a sweetheart," he cooed to the dog, alleviating a little of Kaylee's anguish. He lifted his gaze to her. "I'll be fine. I'd just like you to go now."

Kaylee acquiesced, uncertain what to make of his reaction to her questions. She set Bear in the car. "You saved my bacon back there. Thanks."

Bear cocked his head, apparently fixating on the word bacon.

Kaylee laughed and reached for the dog treats she kept in the glove box. "Yeah, you deserve a treat. Here you go."

Bear settled on the seat and nibbled at his reward.

Kaylee laughed again. She'd never seen a dog eat so daintily. Most seemed to wolf things down in three bites tops.

She headed for Neil Dykstra's home next, which also happened to be the headquarters of his landscape company. Her cell phone rang. Kaylee turned on the speakerphone and kept driving. "Hey, Mary. What's up?"

"I talked to a couple of my law enforcement contacts like you asked."

"And?"

"They mulled my question over for quite a while, said they'd never really thought about the possible significance. They finally admitted that Joelle's father had been in the sheriff's office almost daily demanding updates and results, and then never came in again after Danny was declared missing and their prime suspect."

"Huh. You'd think he'd want to know what they were doing to locate Danny."

"You'd think. They assumed he'd accepted that Danny's capture was out of the local sheriff's hands after that."

"Do they know whether he contacted the FBI?"

"They wondered about that, but if he did, word never got back to the sheriff's office."

Spotting Neil's place a hundred yards ahead, Kaylee pulled to the shoulder to finish their conversation. "Did your contacts mention anyone else? Anyone who continued to press for answers?"

"No, they said Neil didn't before or after Danny disappeared. But he was just a kid."

And was blaming himself, because he was supposed to have been with Joelle that night.

"On the other hand," Mary went on, "Glen Phelps had been in the office a lot complaining about vandalism before Danny disappeared. He'd organized a downtown business association to help push for action and had declared himself their spokesperson. After Danny disappeared, the complaints stopped. But then again, so did the vandalism."

"So Glen had no reason to keep bugging the sheriff. But Walter's withdrawal bothers me. I was just at his place, and he got very agitated when I suggested Danny might not have been the one who caused his daughter's boating accident."

"Wouldn't that bother you? It would mean whoever is responsible is still at large."

"Sure, but until this morning, he would've assumed Danny was too, unless—"

"Unless he already knew Danny was dead," Mary said soberly.

Kaylee's heart tightened. The sun slipped behind a cloud, casting a dark shadow across the road ahead. It was hard to imagine the sweet man who'd taken such a shine to her dog being capable of ending a boy's life. But thirty-five years ago, pain and rage would've been eating him alive.

"Maybe it'd be better to just leave well enough alone," Mary said softly. "The man has suffered enough. If he did have something to do with Danny's demise, doubts about whether the right culprit died will likely torment him more than any punishment the justice system could dole out."

"What about ensuring Joelle's killer is held responsible?"

Mary's heavy sigh filled the car. "We don't know the killer wasn't Danny." Her tone was a mix of exasperation and empathy. "This isn't your fight, Kaylee."

Kaylee's mind knew she was right, but she couldn't let it go. She shifted her gaze heavenward, and it settled on the church steeple rising above the town. *God knows the truth. But is that enough? Doesn't Joelle deserve better?*

As she hung up with Mary, Kaylee saw one of Digger's company trucks turn into his yard. "I think I'll take that as a sign not to give up just yet. What do you think?" she said to Bear.

The little dog roused from his nap and let out a woof.

"Me too." She pulled back onto the road and followed the truck.

Two men piled out of the truck and watched her drive up and climb out of her car. One of them removed his sunglasses and smoothed his wind-tousled dark brown hair with a quick swipe. "How can we help you?"

"I'm looking for Neil Dykstra."

"He'll be a few hours yet. He was headed to Mount Constitution for a hike. Can I help you with anything?"

"Ah, I didn't know he enjoyed hiking. Has he ever been to the Klamath Mountains in Oregon?"

The man gave her a look that indicated he had no idea why she was asking him that, but he answered anyway. "Probably. He's climbed every mountain on the coast from Canada to Mexico."

"And here I'd heard he was more of a water man. A boat racer."

The other crewman, who was probably in his early fifties—closest in age to his boss—scrutinized her suspiciously. "Who are you?"

Kaylee introduced herself.

"We can't help you," the man said tersely, then hefted a bag of soil off the truck and tramped into the utility building.

"Don't mind Bob." The dark-haired man put his sunglasses back on and herded her toward her car. "He and Digger have been friends since they were kids. Doesn't want to see him get into another funk over the old girlfriend. I personally don't understand why Digger still holds such a torch for her. Not when there are plenty of other fish in the sea around here."

Bob emerged from the utility shed. "Randy, I could use a hand here," he barked.

"Sorry about that." Randy held open Kaylee's door for her and grinned at her attempts to keep Bear from wriggling out. "I'll be done in another half hour. If you want to meet for dinner at the Pacific Street Diner around six, maybe I can answer your questions."

"Sure." She was pretty sure it wasn't an altruistic offer, but with any luck he would answer all of her questions. "See you then."

Bear scowled at her the whole way back to the cottage to drop him off.

"Don't give me that. I can't take you everywhere, can I?"

Bear snorted.

Kaylee opened the car door for him. "I'm sorry, buddy. I'll make it up to you."

Bear trotted toward the cottage with his nose in the air.

"Come on, Bear, you know you're my main guy," she teased.

Kaylee put out his food, quickly changed her clothes, and arrived at the Pacific Street Diner three minutes early. There was no sign of Randy at any of the tables, so she waited for him by the door and perused the menu.

Ten minutes later, the waitress offered to seat her, but Kaylee declined.

"I'll give him a few more minutes. Thanks." Kaylee glanced outside, but had no idea what kind of vehicle Randy drove or his cell phone number. For all she knew, the grumpy Bob had overheard his invitation and talked him out of coming to talk to her.

Two women hurried inside and straight to the hostess. "Do you know who owns the red Ford Escape in your back lot?" one asked.

Kaylee whirled around, bracing for the news they'd just backed into it or something. "It's mine. Why?"

"Your tires have been slashed."

5

Kaylee groaned at the sight of her car hunched on its rims.

A metallic *ping* made her jump. She glanced around, but couldn't see anyone in the deepening shadows. It had probably been an engine cooling.

A soft rustle sounded behind her.

She spun in time to see a cat jump out of the Dumpster with a fish head in its mouth. She shook her head. What did she think? That whoever did this to her tires was waiting out here to flatten her too?

Kaylee's heart thudded. Neil's friend Bob hadn't seemed happy about her questions. Nor had Mr. Spiece, for that matter. Not that she could imagine him trailing her here to scare her out of turning up new information on this old case. After one last glance around to ensure no one was waiting to ambush her, she examined each tire. They didn't appear to be slashed, merely deflated. That was a relief anyway.

She peered up the street and calculated the distance to the closest gas station with an air pump—too far to drive her car like this. She dug her phone out of her purse and pulled up a list of garages on the island with tow trucks.

A pickup veered into the parking lot and sped toward her.

Her heart racing, she leapt behind her car.

The pickup skidded to a stop opposite her, and the driver's window whirred down. Randy sat behind the wheel. "Hey, good timing. I thought I was going to be late."

"You are. I've been here for twenty minutes—long enough for someone to let the air out of all my tires."

He laughed. "Don't take it personally. It was probably an initiation prank."

"I didn't think the high school allowed upperclassmen to initiate freshmen with stunts like that anymore."

He hopped out of his truck, grinning. "Like they could stop it." He reached into the giant toolbox in the back of his truck and pulled out a small air compressor. "Don't worry. I can get you driving on air in no time."

A cruiser turned into the parking lot with its lights swirling and parked behind Randy's pickup. Deputy Alan Brooks, a young rookie Kaylee had encountered a few times, hopped out of the cruiser and looked from the flat tires to Kaylee. "This just isn't your week, Miss Bleu."

"Yeah, tell me about it."

He flipped open his notebook. "The restaurant hostess called us. Any idea who might've done this?"

"Randy here"—Kaylee hitched her thumb toward him—"thinks it was an initiation prank."

Deputy Brooks nodded. "Could be. Wouldn't be the first time. More than a few likely go unreported." He noted the time Kaylee parked and the time the women reported seeing the flat tires. "You didn't see anyone lurking around when you arrived?"

"No."

"Anyone have a grudge against you?"

Her earlier fears floated through her mind. They seemed silly now. "Not that I know of."

Randy, crouched beside her back tire, piped up. "If their intent was malicious, they would've slashed the tires, don't you think?"

An indignant tone Kaylee recognized all too well drifted from the sidewalk. "Do you see that?" Mrs. Banks demanded of her daughter in her oh-so-proper tone. "Now something's going on behind the Pacific Street Diner. What's this island coming to?"

"Are we finished?" Kaylee whispered, ducking behind the van next to her. All it would take to lose the wedding contract would be for Mrs. Banks to spot her talking to another deputy about another crime. Never mind that Kaylee was the victim here and an innocent bystander the first time. Mrs. Banks would assume she attracted trouble and would end up involved in some kind of uproar at Chelsea's wedding. Kaylee couldn't really argue with that at this point.

Deputy Brooks examined the tires and ground around her vehicle, made a note in his notebook, then flipped it closed. "Yup, thanks for your time."

Randy appeared from the other side of the car. "There. Tires are good as new." He stuffed his little compressor back in his toolbox. "Ready to eat?"

Kaylee stepped forward to thank him.

"Isn't that the slapdash florist you like?" Mrs. Banks's words pierced the air.

Kaylee shrank back. "Sorry," she whispered to Randy. "I have to go."

"What?" He stared at her, puzzled.

"Uh, could you move your truck so I can pull out?" Kaylee ducked into her car, grateful that she'd forgotten to replace the interior light bulb that had blown last week. She slapped on the baseball cap wedged between the seats. With any luck, Mrs. Banks wouldn't be able to see her through the window.

Randy finally took the hint and moved his truck out of her way. Kaylee couldn't get out of there fast enough.

Kaylee slept fitfully. Dreams about Danny's and Joelle's deaths were interspersed with images of her car tires being thrown in the hole in the shop's side yard, and it was all set to a sound track of Mrs. Banks complaining about how unsuitable Kaylee was to be their florist.

She awoke with a start at the thought that she was late for their meeting at the country club. Except, no, today was Sunday. The meeting wasn't for another day.

Bear stirred at the end of the bed.

"Sorry. Bad dream." She squinted at her clock. Ten more minutes before the alarm was set to ring. She turned it off and closed her eyes again to snatch a few more minutes' rest.

The cry of a gull jerked her awake half an hour later. "Ah! Bear, get up. You don't have much time to go outside before I have to leave."

Bear jumped down and scrambled across the kitchen, beating her to the side door by a tail.

"Good boy." She pushed open the door. "Don't be long." Glancing at the clock, she repeated the admonition to herself as she clicked on the coffee maker and then jumped in the shower.

When she flung back the shower curtain a few minutes later, the aroma of brewing coffee spurred her on. She threw on the black leggings and tunic she'd set out the night before—dressy enough for Sunday service and still casual enough for the youth event afterward. She popped a couple slices of bread into the toaster, filled Bear's bowl with kibble, then opened the door. "Breakfast is ready, buddy."

Bear didn't come running. She never should've told him she was leaving. Not that it mattered. He seemed to know when it was Sunday and would dawdle all he wanted because he knew she'd be leaving him at home. She left the door ajar and quickly ate her toast and coffee.

She called for him out the door again. When he still didn't come, she locked the side door, grabbed her jacket and purse, and went out the front door. Standing on the porch, she jangled her car keys. "Bear?"

He burst out from under one of the bushes, a slobbery piece of paper crunched in his mouth.

"Have you been getting into my wastebasket again? That better not be something important." She reached out her hand and he dropped the paper. Pasted-on newsprint letters filled the page. Her stomach lurched as she flattened out the sheet.

Poke around where you shouldn't, pay the price.

"Where did you find this?" Kaylee demanded of her dog, receiving only a faint whine in response. She assessed the note. The top right corner of the page was torn. Kaylee glanced around and found it at the base of the screen door. "Was the note caught in the screen door?"

Bear tilted his head, his ears perked.

She'd let him out the side door earlier. She had also come in that way last night because she'd carried the garbage can in from the road. So the page could've been in the door since sometime yesterday. She shivered at the thought of some creep lurking out here while she was sleeping.

She checked the time on her phone. "And I'm really late. Let's go." She slid the note into the outside pocket of her purse, then hurried to her car with Bear on her heels.

As she backed out of the driveway, she had the hair-raising feeling she was being watched. She pulled onto the road and watched her rearview mirror. No sign of anyone tailing her. Her mind flashed to last night's flattened tires. The work of the same person?

Neil's friend Bob hadn't been thrilled about her asking questions and had probably heard Randy's invitation to dinner.

Then again, she couldn't see Bob taking the time to cut out letters to send her a threatening note.

"I'm being paranoid," she said to Bear. She slammed on the brakes. "What am I doing? You can't come to church." She pulled a U-turn. "That note has me all frazzled." She parked in front of the cottage and escorted Bear inside. Making her anxious was probably exactly what the note writer had wanted. "Well it won't work," she said to the yard and anyone who might be listening as she climbed back into her car. *If someone feels the need to intimidate me, it must mean I'm onto something. Right?*

Kaylee arrived at church without remembering the drive.

Jessica stopped her outside the sanctuary doors. "What's wrong? You're shaking."

Kaylee glanced at her trembling hands and let out a sigh. "You got a few minutes?"

"Of course." Jessica guided her to a quiet corner of the foyer. "Did something happen?"

Kaylee pulled the note from her purse. "Bear found this stuck in my front door this morning."

Jessica gasped. "Did you call the sheriff's office?"

"No. I was already running late."

Jessica glanced around the foyer and then scanned the rows of parked cars through the window. "And it doesn't look as if Deputy Skenandore is here today. His granddaughters are visiting for the weekend, so they probably came to the early service. Any idea who sent the note?"

"Uh, yeah. Danny's murderer."

Jessica winced. "Maybe not. After you left the bakery yesterday, more than a few people muttered disapproval of our stirring up unfounded speculation."

"Do you think I should keep out of it? Stop asking questions? Mary seems to."

A couple shot them sideways glances across the foyer, then whispered to each other.

"I don't know what to think," Jessica said as DeeDee joined them.

"Think about what?" DeeDee asked.

Kaylee showed her the note.

"Cut-and-paste notes are usually the work of a woman," DeeDee said authoritatively, although Kaylee was a tad dubious of her sources—mainly mystery novels.

In a vain effort to tame her zigzagging thoughts, Kaylee rearranged the plants in the urn next to where they were standing. "The only woman who has a stake in keeping me from investigating is Chelsea, because her mother threatened to make her go to a more suitable florist."

"The note sounds like something Glen Phelps would say," Jessica said.

"Have you seen him lately?" Kaylee said. "His hands are riddled with arthritis. There's no way he could cut and paste those letters."

DeeDee was still carefully studying the note. "And these letters aren't from the Orcas Island paper either. It's the wrong font."

The worship music started.

"We better get in there," Jessica said. "We can talk more about this after the service."

"Actually I volunteered to help with the youth outing after church." Kaylee took the note from DeeDee and stuffed it back in her purse. She followed her friends and their husbands inside. Thankfully the music and message soon swept away her anxious thoughts.

The moment Kaylee and her friends stepped out of the service, DeeDee's two girls, Polly and Zoe, surrounded them, showing off the crafts they'd made in Sunday school.

"C'mon, girls," DeeDee said. "Let Kaylee breathe. Grandma's expecting us for lunch." To Kaylee she added, "Call me later if you need to talk."

Kaylee thanked her and Jessica, who seemed reluctant to leave without doing something about the note. "I'll be fine," Kaylee said, despite the twinge in her stomach that suggested otherwise.

6

The three bubbly girls in Kaylee's backseat—Maggie, Jenna, and Cassidy—banished concerns about the note sender from Kaylee's mind. After all, she'd be surrounded by dozens of youth and volunteers all afternoon at Turtle Cove Town Park.

Some of the teens drove their own vehicles to the park. Some rode bicycles. The rest carpooled with volunteers like Kaylee. "What do you girls want to do first when we get there?" Kaylee asked her group. The park boasted a skate park, tennis courts, a basketball court, baseball diamonds, and a playground.

"Eat," Cassidy said. "I'm starving."

"I'm sure the grill masters will be pumping out hot dogs in no time." Kaylee had hoped the group would vote to go hiking at the wildlife preserve, but the majority had opted for an afternoon baseball game against a youth group from Deer Harbor. Those who didn't enjoy playing could cheer on their friends or enjoy the other activities the park had to offer.

The girls raced off the instant Kaylee parked. Kaylee spotted Reese firing up a barbecue and meandered over. "How can I help?"

"There are drinks and condiments in there"—he pointed to a cooler—"and buns and chips in there"—he pointed to a large cardboard box. "Do you mind setting everything out on the picnic table?"

"No problem. That's what I'm here for."

"Thanks." His smile said he was happy to see her here.

The gang devoured lunch in record time and then the games began. Kaylee joined the players on the field, but two of her carpool girls opted to watch from the sidelines. Halfway into the second inning, a third girl Kaylee didn't recognize joined them, seeming perturbed.

Kaylee jogged over to the group as her team came off the field to end the inning. "Everything okay?"

"I'm going to go for a ride," the newcomer said, climbing on a bike.

"Isn't that one of the boys' bikes?" Kaylee asked.

"Yeah," Cassidy spoke up. "Matt's."

"Don't worry," the new girl said. "I'll be back before the game's over. He won't even miss it."

"Nevertheless," Kaylee said, "you need to make sure he doesn't mind you borrowing it."

The girl let out an irritated-sounding huff. "Hey, Matt, can I take your bike for a spin around the park?"

He waved to her and she took off.

"She's super annoyed with Matt," Cassidy said. "He invited her to come out today and has ignored her all afternoon."

"I think she assumed he was interested in dating her," Jenna added, "so I told her he's just really friendly and is always inviting people to events when he thinks they'll enjoy them."

"Ah." Kaylee took a swig of water from her bottle as she watched the girl speed into the wooded area on the far side of the next diamond. She must've run into mud, because the bike skidded out. Kaylee started toward her, but the girl picked up the bike and, with a quick glance over her shoulder, probably hoping no one had spotted her, took off again.

"How's it going?" Reese asked from behind her.

"Peachy," she said, turning to beam at him.

He held up a bat. "Good, because it's your turn to hit."

By the time the game was over and Kaylee returned to the table where Cassidy and Jenna were still sitting, Matt's bicycle was back. The bike looked a little worse for wear, and the girl who'd borrowed it was nowhere in sight.

"She walked home," Cassidy said, apparently reading Kaylee's thoughts.

"Did she tell him she bent the back rod?" Kaylee pointed.

"Nah. She tried to get his attention when she got back, but when Matt's playing a game, he zones everything else out. He probably won't even remember anyone asked to borrow the bike."

"Whose bike?" Matt asked, hiking a leg over the seat.

"Yours," Kaylee said.

"Someone borrowed my bike?" He glanced over it and didn't seem to notice anything amiss.

"I'm afraid she damaged it a bit too." Kaylee pointed to the bent rod.

"Nah, I did that last week. Haven't had time to fix it yet. Later." He rode off.

Kaylee drove the girls home, then headed back to Wildflower Cottage. The serene rural setting in the shadow of Turtleback Mountain usually filled her with peace, but as she neared the little cottage she'd bought from her grandmother, her thoughts returned to the note Bear found that morning and her senses went on high alert.

She peered around as she turned into the driveway, but couldn't see any cars or bicycles lurking nearby. She let Bear out and walked the perimeter of the house, then the yard. Bear didn't react oddly to any smells he was picking up.

Kaylee spotted her neighbor from down the road, Tracy Joplin, walking past. "Hi, Tracy. Did you happen to see anyone at my place yesterday afternoon or evening? Or early this morning?"

Tracy shook her head. "No. I haven't heard any cars either. Why?"

"Someone left me a note, but forgot to sign it," Kaylee said.

She didn't want to unnecessarily worry the woman, since her daughter, Bridget, loved to come play with Bear.

Leaving Tracy to her walk, Kaylee returned to the cottage and scrutinized the doors and windows. "It doesn't look as if anyone tried to get in," she said to Bear. *Thank goodness.* All she wanted to do was relax. Muscles she didn't remember having ached. Showing the note to the sheriff could wait until tomorrow.

Monday morning, Kaylee awoke with a nervous flutter in her stomach that had less to do with the note Bear had found than with the day's looming main event. Today was her best chance to finally win over Mrs. Banks in their meeting at the country club. "I was less nervous the day I had to defend my doctoral thesis to a room full of professors," Kaylee said to Bear.

But graduate school had taught her plant taxonomy, not how to reconcile accounts and keep customers happy. She still had a lot to learn when it came to running The Flower Patch. She consciously shoved aside the nagging thought that maybe she didn't have what it took to keep the florist shop solvent, no matter how much she enjoyed running it. She needed to focus on what lay ahead.

Sighing, Kaylee took extra care with her makeup and clothes so she'd look the part of a florist worthy of the country club crowd's patronage, even though everything in her rebelled at the idea. She preferred to let her work speak for itself, and this wasn't the first time she'd done arrangements for the venue.

But with the unexpected plumbing bill coming in and the potential negative ripple effect of a yard cordoned off with police tape for who knows how long, she couldn't afford to lose Mrs.

Banks's favor. Not if the wealthy woman had half the influence she claimed over the rest of her society friends.

Kaylee fortified herself with a full breakfast, then glanced at the time and squeaked. It was much later than she'd thought. "We gotta go!"

This time, Bear was ready and waiting.

As Kaylee pulled up next to the shop ten minutes later, a young couple was turning away from the locked door. "I'll be right there," Kaylee called out, then grabbed her purse.

As soon as the car door was open, Bear hopped out and raced ahead of her.

"Sorry I'm late," Kaylee said as she unlocked the door. She was grateful that it was locked and there were no creepy notes shoved in it.

The couple asked what was going on in the side yard, to which Kaylee said as little as possible. As they browsed the shop, one of the guys from animal control who'd captured her rogue snake walked in.

"I was passing through, so I thought I'd give you the good news in person," he said. "That snake in your plant wasn't poisonous."

The couple's attention snapped their way.

"A hitchhiker in one of my shipments," Kaylee explained to them with a smile.

The woman eyeballed the planters nearest her and moved closer to her husband.

"It was just a corn snake," the animal control worker went on. "They are quite docile, prefer not to bite if they can avoid it, and actually make popular pets."

The woman pushed away the assorted planter her husband held and whispered feverishly to him. They hustled out of the shop.

Kaylee's sigh must've been more audible than she'd thought,

because the worker from animal control apologized. "I guess that news would've been better shared in private."

"It's okay. I'm glad to hear we were never in danger. And my customers need never know." She hoped.

She glanced out the front window as he exited.

The couple who'd been browsing moments earlier were talking to someone on the sidewalk and glancing back at the shop. *Terrific.* By suppertime, the little corn snake episode could easily be a tale of epic proportions.

Kaylee slipped outside to fish the water hose back through the bathroom window. It flopped against her leg, leaving a black mark on her pants. "Oh great. Just the kind of thing Mrs. Banks is bound to notice."

Jessica appeared carrying a cup of coffee and held it out to Kaylee. "I saw you rushing in this morning and figured you could use this."

"Thank you." Kaylee cupped it with both hands and took a long sip.

"You didn't call me last night. I hope that means there weren't any more nasty surprises waiting for you when you got home."

"Not a one."

"What did the sheriff say about the note?" Jessica asked.

Kaylee ducked her head. "I haven't called him yet."

"You need to do that sooner rather than later," Jessica scolded.

"I'll stop by his office after Mary gets in. I have another appointment that way this afternoon."

"Make sure you do."

"I did get some good news this morning. If you want to call it that." Kaylee told Jessica about the corn snake.

Jessica raised an eyebrow. "I heard the son of the new flower shop owner has a pet snake. Maybe he dropped one in your shop to scare customers his mom's way."

Kaylee shook her head. "I'm pretty sure I would've noticed if a teenager had walked in with a snake."

"You never know," Jessica said in that tone she slipped into when imagining a new conspiracy.

"Jess, if you're trying to make me feel better, it's not working."

"Sorry. I can't help myself. I'll see you later." She headed back to her shop and Kaylee finished dragging the hose into the bathroom for easy access.

Mary rushed into The Flower Patch. "Sorry I'm late. You better run."

"Run where?"

"Your appointment with Chelsea Banks. It's been switched to eleven. Didn't you see my note?"

Kaylee's pulse jumped. "I haven't even been to the desk yet." She gaped around wildly. "The plants still need to be watered." She straightened her top and patted her hair. "How do I look?"

"Great. You'll be fine."

"Thanks for coming in early. I'll be back as soon as I can." Kaylee rushed out and headed to the country club in the shop van. No point in risking Chelsea's mom recognizing Kaylee's red Ford Escape from the parking lot Saturday night.

Halfway to the country club, a dark sedan appeared in her rearview mirror. Three turns later, it was still there.

She pulled into Turtleback Country Club's parking lot. So did the driver of the sedan, who parked in the back corner of the lot.

Kaylee waited in the van to see if the driver headed in, but to no avail. Whoever was in the sedan was staying put.

Five minutes later, not wanting to be late for her appointment with Chelsea, Kaylee climbed out. She took a few steps toward the clubhouse, then muttered, "This is crazy." She spun around and stalked toward the mystery sedan.

The way the sun hit the windshield made it impossible to

see the driver until she was within six feet of the car. *Raylene?* Kaylee walked over to the open window, her trepidation easing. "Hey, what brings you here?"

"A lunch meeting with the congressman."

"Ah." No wonder she was hanging back in the car. It was more than an hour until lunchtime. In the meantime, she seemed to be working on whatever it was she did for the congressman on a small tablet on her lap. "I have an appointment with a wedding client." Kaylee glanced at her watch. "In three minutes. Got to dash."

Mrs. Banks frowned at Kaylee as she entered the lobby.

Kaylee lifted her chin and smiled. "Good morning," she said brightly.

"We'll see. This way." Mrs. Banks led the way to the largest dining room.

Kaylee managed to snatch a glimpse of her appearance as they passed a mirror and decided it passed muster. Even the mark on her pants was scarcely visible. Mrs. Banks was just being Mrs. Banks.

Forty-five minutes later, Kaylee felt she had impressed Chelsea and Mrs. Banks with her proposal, complete with photographs of comparable arbors she'd used at previous venues. She made a point of emphasizing that Chelsea's would, of course, be unique. With each new suggestion for the room's various nooks, her confidence that she'd secured the contract grew.

Then Raylene strolled in.

Mrs. Banks yoo-hooed her over, clearly intent on wowing Kaylee with her connections to Congressman Munk. "Miss Nelson, have you met our florist, Kaylee Bleu?" To Kaylee, she added, "Miss Nelson is Congressman Munk's right hand."

Kaylee smiled sweetly. "Yes, we've met. Nice to see you again, Raylene."

"Have the police finally cleared up that nasty business in your yard?" Raylene asked.

Mrs. Banks visibly cringed.

Kaylee managed to keep her smile in place. "I've been assured it will be soon."

"That must be a relief for you," Raylene said, her tone saccharine. "It probably raised a few eyebrows amongst potential customers." She nodded to Mrs. Banks and then found herself a seat.

Mrs. Banks pulled her daughter aside and addressed her in a whisper that Kaylee couldn't help but overhear. "See what I mean? Miss Nelson personally knows this florist you picked and still implied others would question my judgment in using her, thanks to this business in her yard."

"Mother, that is *not* what she said," Chelsea argued.

Mrs. Banks shushed her daughter with a flutter of hands. "I've made my decision."

Kaylee braced for the news, telling herself to accept it with grace.

Ignoring her daughter's continuing protests, Mrs. Banks stepped up to Kaylee. "Thank you for your time, but I don't think your designs are a good fit for us."

A deep male chuckle split the air.

"Congressman Munk, hello." Mrs. Banks's voice was suddenly sticky-sweet. "How nice to see you."

"Delores, do you know who you're turning down?" Ted said in a stage whisper as he approached. He shot Kaylee a conspiratorial wink. "Once I'm elected, I intend to make Ms. Bleu here the exclusive florist to the governor's mansion."

Mrs. Banks gasped. "I had no idea." She looked at Kaylee with a hungry gleam in her eye. "Then of course we must have her. Only the best for our Chelsea."

Kaylee whipped out the contract she'd prepared. "That's fine. If you could just sign and date here"—she pointed to the bottom of the page—"and supply the listed nonrefundable deposit, we'll be all set to proceed."

Ted appeared impressed by her move, and she tossed him a smile.

Five minutes later, Kaylee had a signed contract and a check in hand, and Mrs. Banks was twittering animatedly to anyone who would listen about how she was using the future governor's florist for her daughter's wedding.

Kaylee hugged her clipboard to her chest and beamed up at Ted. "Thank you."

He grinned. "You can thank me by playing a round of golf with me."

Her heart skipped a beat. Was he asking her on a date? Out of the corner of her eye, she caught Raylene scowling. Kaylee had enough reasons of her own to hesitate. She glanced out the picture windows at the fairways beyond. "It's been years since I played."

"It'll be fun," he insisted.

His warm brown eyes and earnest expression coaxed her into nodding in agreement.

"Terrific. Does tomorrow afternoon at three work for you?"

"Sure. I'll see you then."

"I'll pick you up. At Wildflower Cottage?"

Kaylee's heart stuttered at the fact that he knew where she lived. She'd taken over her grandmother's shop. Of course he'd assume she had moved into her grandmother's house as well.

She shook her head. "I'll be at The Flower Patch."

"Great. I'll drop by there for you."

On her way back to the shop van, Kaylee couldn't help but wonder exactly what she'd just agreed to doing.

7

The next morning, Kaylee arrived at the shop to the fantastic sight of George working on her new well pump. She'd called him the minute she'd heard from Sheriff Maddox that he had released her yard. "How's the pump coming along?" she asked George.

"Should have your water running by lunchtime."

She gave him a huge smile. "Thank you so much. I appreciate you coming over extra early this morning."

With a wave, Kaylee let herself in the side door and dove into finalizing the plans for Chelsea's floral arrangements.

She had a couple of walk-in customers who each purchased small arrangements, but the shop was otherwise quiet that morning.

As promised, George had her water flowing with half an hour to spare before lunch, and he headed out with a promise to send someone over soon to fill the hole.

Kaylee breathed a sigh of relief. The sooner the hole was out of sight, the sooner it—and everything connected to it—would be out of customers' minds.

Within moments of George's departure, Mary sauntered in with the bag of golf clubs Kaylee had asked to borrow. "Someone's happy."

Kaylee couldn't hold back the smile that tugged at her lips. "The sun's shining. I have my yard back. And our water is flowing again."

"And you have a date with a certain handsome congressman." Mary set her golf bag in the back hall.

"It's hardly a date. The man only spends a few weeks a year on the island. It's not as if he's interested in anything serious."

"That's not what I heard." Mary's tone implied Kaylee had been holding out on her. "There's a rumor going around that you're to be the florist to the governor's office if he wins the election."

"He said that so Mrs. Banks would hire us."

"Uh-huh. Well, let's hope he follows through if he wins, or Mrs. Banks will be starting rumors about how he dumped you."

"She wouldn't dare. Not after I've done her daughter's wedding. She'd twist the story better than the governor's spin doctors and make us both come out smelling like roses."

Mary laughed. "That's so true." She glanced around. "Where's Bear?"

"I left him at home since I'll be out all afternoon at the golf course, and then we have our Petal Pushers meeting tonight. The girl down the street is going to stop by and let him out."

Mary's eyes twinkled. "You really think you'll make it to the Petal Pushers meeting?"

Kaylee rolled her eyes. "It's not a date."

"Whatever you say." Mary scrutinized the list of arrangements on her week's to-do list. "Did you hear that Sheriff Maddox ruled Danny Lane's death accidental and closed the case?"

"What? How could he come to that conclusion so soon?"

"I thought you'd be happy he wrapped the whole thing up."

"For the business sure, but I'm not convinced Danny's death was an accident. Why else would someone send me that note?" She slapped a hand to her forehead. "I should've called the sheriff about that sooner. I just got so busy yesterday."

"Jess and DeeDee told me about the note. DeeDee might be right about it being from Glen Phelps. The way he blabbed about Bea, I was getting worried they'd drag her up from Arizona to question her."

"Question her about what?"

"Glen said she'd had run-ins with Danny over previous incidents at the shop."

"Well, I'm glad the sheriff had the good sense not to suspect her of taking revenge on the boy. She wouldn't hurt a fly."

As if her grandmother had heard them talking about her, Bea chose that moment to call the shop. Kaylee tried to downplay the events of the past few days, but her grandmother had obviously been talking to other islanders.

"I wanted you to know that those rumors about me are hogwash," Bea said.

"I never doubted that for a second, Grandma."

"Good. I cried my heart out when I heard that poor boy fell in the hole and died."

Kaylee's heart twisted at the anguish in her grandmother's voice.

"He was a good boy," Bea went on. "Sure I caught him pinching a rose one day. But it was for a girl he liked, and he didn't have two pennies to rub together. So I offered him a job weeding to earn some money."

Kaylee grinned. That sounded like her grandmother.

"I'll tell you another thing. There is no way Danny caused that boating accident like they said. Like I told old Sheriff Wilson all those years ago, Danny was afraid to go on the water. He nearly drowned as a youngster. And I told the sheriff Danny wouldn't have left the island without saying goodbye to me either, let alone without picking up his paycheck. But the man wouldn't listen."

"Neither will Sheriff Maddox."

"You have to make him," Bea insisted. "I always had a bad feeling Danny had come to harm, but I couldn't even get the boy's father to believe me. I should've done more."

"It sounds as if you did more than anyone."

"Promise me you won't let Sheriff Maddox give up on getting to the truth this time."

Kaylee sighed. "I'm doing my best."

"I knew I could count on you." Bea's voice cracked, then became brisk again as usual. "Well, listen to me nattering on. I need to let you get back to work."

"I'll talk to you soon."

As Kaylee hung up, Mary said, "I guess this clinches your decision to keep digging into this mystery."

"You should've heard her. The idea that Danny killed someone—accidentally or not—is too horrible for her to believe. And she's heartbroken over his death."

Mary frowned. "I never thought about how heavily that would weigh on her."

"I'm glad she doesn't seem to believe it's true."

"I noticed you didn't tell her about your golf date."

Kaylee blinked at the shift in subject. "Well, I wasn't sure what she'd think of me playing hooky from the shop for most of the afternoon."

Mary laughed. "The thrill of knowing you're going out on a date would more than get you off the hook. It's working with me."

"You're probably right." Kaylee glanced outside and saw a familiar figure heading around the side of the building with a shovel. Grateful for a reason to escape, she excused herself and stepped out the side door. "Hey, Reese. You don't need to do that. George was going to send someone."

"I volunteered."

"How thoughtful."

He grinned at her. "Always happy to help."

Kaylee opened her mouth to say more, but she was interrupted.

"Kaylee!" Mary's voice drifted out the door. "Your golf date's here."

Reese's shovel jerked, missing the clump of dirt he'd been aiming for. "You golf?"

Kaylee shrugged. "Not really. The congressman saved me from losing a big contract yesterday, and playing a round of golf with him was all he asked in return." She wasn't really sure why she felt the compulsion to explain, except that here Reese was working in her yard while she went off to play.

"Oh, a game of golf is the going rate for gratitude?" Reese's tone was teasing as he attacked the dirt with vigor. "I've been undershooting with just dinner then."

"Kaylee, did you hear me?" Mary called louder.

"I'm coming," Kaylee called. To Reese, she said, "I better go."

Reese waved distractedly, apparently completely focused on filling the hole.

Ted already had the borrowed clubs slung over his shoulder by the time Kaylee got back to the front of the shop. He motioned her ahead of him out the door, where a red Mustang convertible sat at the curb. "I love driving with the top down. Do you mind?" he asked as he opened the passenger door for her.

"I don't know. I've never ridden in a convertible."

He plopped her clubs in the trunk. "Then you're in for a treat."

As he set out, the wind caught her hair and slapped it across her face. Laughing, she tamed it into a ponytail with an elastic band. The adventure turned less amusing when Ted hit the edge of town and picked up speed on the country roads, swerving recklessly. Kaylee closed her eyes and tried to think about something else.

Ten minutes later, Ted pulled into the country club's parking lot and swept open her door once more. "So? What did you think?"

"I'm not sure 'treat' is the word I'd use."

He shrugged. "I guess it's not for everybody." He retrieved

her golf clubs from the trunk and then motioned her onward. "The wind noise does make it hard to hold a conversation. But it's great for thinking."

That it is. She'd been thinking how to ask the congressman to use his clout to ensure Danny Lane's death was more thoroughly investigated. After all her grandmother had done for her, not blindly accepting the easy answer to something that was important to Bea was the least she could do in return.

As they passed by the front entrance of the country club, a familiar voice called out, "Hey, Kaylee."

"Hi, Randy," Kaylee said. She had been so absorbed in her thoughts she hadn't noticed the landscaping crew arranging large boulders in the gardens flanking the doors. She noticed the rest of the crew, recognizing one of them. "Hey, Bob."

Bob scowled at her, then at Randy.

"Hey, Digger. Oh, sorry. You go by Neil these days, don't you?" Ted said to a worker Kaylee recognized from the photos in Mr. Spiece's house. He was older, but it was definitely the same guy. "Looks as if business is good."

Neil scarcely glanced up from what he was doing. "Not bad."

"Neil? I'm Kaylee Bleu," she said. "I own the Flower Patch."

"You need some landscaping done?" he asked.

"Uh no. I imagine you've heard—"

"Ma'am, we're kinda busy here, and I *imagine* you have a tee time to make."

"Yes, sorry. Perhaps we can talk some other time."

Neil didn't respond.

Ted clasped her elbow. "Let's go." To Neil he said, "Good to see you again."

Neil's snort didn't sound as if he shared the sentiment. Equally likely was that he wasn't happy to see Kaylee. Bob must have told him about her coming around asking questions.

"Not a friendly sort, is he?" she said to Ted once they'd put some distance between themselves and Neil.

Ted chuckled. "Don't take it personally. It's me he doesn't like. We were rivals in high school. I beat him out for quarterback on the football team. I guess it still bugs him."

Kaylee recalled Mary's comment about Ted's love of winning and wondered if Neil would really hold a grudge all these years. If so, he'd probably be even less eager to talk to her about his girlfriend's boating accident now that he'd seen her with Ted. She muffled a sigh.

As Ted visited the men's locker room to change into his golfing shoes, Kaylee perused the annual club champions' pictures lining the hallway. Theodore Munk—an older version of Ted—was labeled as the seniors champion ten years ago.

When Ted emerged from the locker room, Kaylee pointed to the photograph. "Is this your father?"

"It sure is. And when I was a teen, he won the men's club championship." Ted strolled down the hall and stopped in front of a picture of a younger image of his dad holding a massive trophy. A teenage boy stood in the background.

"Is that you standing behind him?"

"No. That was his caddy." Ted glanced at his watch. "We'd better hurry. I need to make sure one of the shop boys has pulled my clubs from storage and has our cart ready for us."

"Did you ever try for the club championship?" Kaylee asked, picking up her pace to keep up with him.

"Yup, I was the junior club champion my last two years before college." He grinned proudly.

She laughed. "Your peers must've hated you—always winning everything."

"Yeah," he said jovially. "They probably just hung around with me for the girls."

Athletic, smart, handsome, and wealthy—not to mention confident. She imagined the girls hung around him in droves.

As they approached the first tee, Kaylee cringed at the number of people standing around watching. It was bad enough Ted would see her miss the ball without two dozen other members witnessing it too. She scrutinized the group. At least Mrs. Banks wasn't among them. She probably couldn't abide a florist who made a fool of herself golfing any more than one who dared have human remains dug from her yard.

Fortunately, Kaylee's first shot went long and straight.

Ted seemed impressed. "I thought you said you haven't played in years."

"I haven't. But I couldn't very well make you look bad by association in front of your fellow members, could I?"

He laughed. "You're priceless."

Kaylee's heart beat a little faster at his warm tone and his light touch on the small of her back as he led her to their golf cart. Was he interested in her?

Did she want him to be?

Not really. His life was on the mainland, in politics. Hanging out in Turtle Cove was nothing more than a temporary diversion. No, she definitely did not want him to be interested. Maybe she needed to start sandbagging every hole to prove their incompatibility.

Between shots, Ted said, "So tell me about yourself. What did you do before you took over your grandmother's flower shop?"

She told him about her career as a forensic botanist. She shared stories about a couple of the cases she'd consulted on for the police, trying to segue into her concerns about the sheriff's abrupt closure of Danny's case. But each time she started to talk about how her grandmother didn't believe Danny's death was an accident or that he could've killed Joelle, she and Ted would have to stop talking to take a shot, and then the congressman would ask Kaylee a question about something totally different.

After five holes of that, Kaylee teed up her ball for the next hole and then stopped and peered over at him. "There's something I've been wanting to ask you, so I'm just going to ask."

His head tilted curiously. "Shoot."

She gulped. Did he mean take her shot and stop holding up the game? Or ask her question?

"Your question?" he prodded.

"As a congressman, I imagine you have a bit of pull with the sheriff's department?"

Ted's eyes twinkled. "Do you have some parking tickets you need me to fix?"

"Not exactly." She glanced at the foursome leaving the green behind them and knew that they would soon be breathing down her neck. "I think the sheriff's conclusions about Danny Lane's death were hasty and unsubstantiated. I'd like you to urge him to reopen the investigation."

Ted's expression turned thoughtful. "I see."

The group on their tails buzzed up to the tee.

The congressman nodded toward her ball. "Take your shot and we can talk as we drive." Once they'd put a couple of shots between them and the players behind them, Ted returned to her question. "I suspect Maddox has examined the incident from far more angles than you realize. He wouldn't arrive at such a conclusion lightly."

"Yes, but I don't see how he could possibly arrive at an authoritative conclusion in such a short amount of time."

Ted glanced over at her and shook his head. "You're an enigma."

"Is that a compliment?" She couldn't decipher his answering smile.

"The truth is, after meeting you in your shop the day of the discovery, I asked Maddox to do his best to wrap up the case quickly for the sake of your business," he said.

"You did?" Butterflies took a test flight through her middle. First he saved her job with Mrs. Banks, now this? Ted Munk was turning out to be a regular knight in shining armor.

"I did. And perhaps I can set your mind at ease about his conclusions. I know it isn't what your grandmother will want to hear, but I was around the same age as Danny, and I remember the speculation that abounded after Joelle's death. Danny had a reputation for being a troublemaker. It didn't surprise anyone that he'd steal a boat to take it out for a joyride."

"But—"

Ted interrupted her. "The truth is, my dad caught him trying to take out one of our boats once."

"Your dad must've been mistaken. My grandmother says Danny was afraid of water."

"Probably a story he spun so she'd be on his side. Trust me. I have no doubt the sheriff's version of what happened thirty-five years ago is correct." Ted's firm tone indicated that he considered the case quite closed.

It looked like it was up to Kaylee to find justice for Danny and Joelle.

8

As the game wore on, Kaylee mulled over Ted's insistence that the sheriff was right about Danny. She watched him putt easily on their tenth hole and would have applauded his birdie, but she was too distracted to muster the energy.

Finally, unable to keep her concerns to herself, she asked, "If you're so sure the sheriff is right, then why is someone afraid of what I'll dig up?"

Ted seemed taken aback. "What do you mean?"

"Someone left an anonymous note at my door Sunday morning. It said, 'Poke around where you shouldn't, pay the price.'"

Ted frowned as he climbed into the golf cart. "Did you tell Maddox?"

"No. I haven't had a chance."

He tapped his foot on the floorboard of the cart, looking increasingly agitated. "You have to be careful with nutjobs like that."

Kaylee sank her putt, then rejoined him in the golf cart. "I imagine politicians get letters like this on a weekly basis, huh?"

"Oh yeah." He gritted his teeth, clearly speaking from personal experience. "Most are empty threats. But it only takes one psycho."

"So you believe me now? Danny's killer must still be on the island and is afraid I'll identify him."

"No, I doubt that." Ted jerked the golf cart to a stop near the next tee. "Law enforcement considers the death an accident. Why risk changing their mind by threatening you?"

"Maybe he didn't know the investigation's status." By this

point, Kaylee had certainly lost interest in finishing the game, but she dutifully climbed out and took her next shot.

"It sounds to me as if you have a sick person toying with you. You need to be careful." Ted yanked a driver from his golf bag with more force than was strictly necessary.

Kaylee shivered. She'd consulted on a serial killer case in her former job, and she knew more than she wanted to about how sick people could be.

Ted teed off, then jammed his club back into his bag. "Maybe we should get you a better dog."

"What's wrong with my dog?"

"A dachshund isn't much of a guard dog."

A smile teased Kaylee's lips at an image of Bear surprising an intruder. "I'm sure it won't come to that."

"If you keep asking people about Danny it might," Ted said.

What did he mean by that? Kaylee clenched her driver in a death grip and gave herself a silent pep talk as she walked to the tee. She was not going to let the note writer, whoever he was, intimidate her. Her grandmother needed to know the truth, and Danny deserved justice.

She teed off and was fairly pleased with her shot. She joined Ted in the cart, and they fell silent as he drove them to the green.

As Kaylee pulled out her putter, the hair on the back of her neck bristled. She glanced around. The green was near the clubhouse, thanks to the serpentine way the fairways ran, but she couldn't spot Neil or any of his men giving her the evil eye. She glanced up to the clubhouse balcony, expecting to see Mrs. Banks.

Raylene, Ted's assistant, stared down at her, or at least in their general direction. From this distance, it was difficult to tell exactly whom she was watching. The assistant sat with her laptop open at a table on the balcony overlooking the green. And she didn't seem the least bit startled by Kaylee spotting her.

"Does your assistant always hang out at the golf club while you're playing a round?" Kaylee asked, jerking her chin toward Raylene.

Ted squinted up and chuckled. "Some days she takes her job a little too seriously. But she's good at it. She can make lemonade out of any lemon we're tossed."

"And do you often run into lemons on the golf course?" Kaylee bit her tongue, fearing she sounded like a jealous girlfriend.

"You'd be surprised the places where problems crop up," he said.

For the next two holes, their conversation didn't venture to anything heavier than favorite foods. Their earlier conversation must've been weighing on Ted's mind, however, because he suddenly said, "How about you let me hire a private investigator to check into who sent you that note?"

She gaped at him. "You'd do that for me?"

"Of course. I don't want you in danger."

"Fore!" somebody shouted.

Before Kaylee could react, Ted pushed her head down and shielded both of them with his arms.

A golf ball plopped on the ground two feet away.

Heart pounding, Kaylee stuttered her thanks. "I . . . I forgot that 'fore' was code for 'duck, ball heading your way.'" Her legs had turned to jelly.

Ted caught her by the arm and propped her up. "You okay?"

"Yes," she said, sounding a little stunned even to her own ears. That ball would have beaned her if not for Ted's quick reaction.

Her game went downhill from there. Her ball found every rough, every sand trap, and every water hole. By the seventeenth hole, Ted seemed as anxious as she was to be finished. She couldn't blame him. Standing around watching someone try to shoot her way out of hazards while the team behind you waited impatiently got old pretty quick.

Her next shot landed next to a low farm fence at the course's boundary. As she approached her ball, her heart jumped. *Picea breweriana* cones lay on the ground. She looked up, stunned to see a large Brewer's spruce on the edge of the neighboring rural property. It appeared to be at least fifty years old, which meant it would've been there when Danny was alive. So much for narrowing down her suspects to people who'd been to the Klamath Mountains.

"Problem?" Ted asked.

"No, sorry. It's just this kind of *Picea* . . . spruce isn't supposed to grow here."

"I guess no one ever told it that." He winked.

She chipped her ball onto the green and lined up her putt, but her thoughts kept returning to that cone she'd seen beneath the folds of Danny's jacket. "Do you know who owned the property next door thirty-five years ago?"

"Thirty-five years ago?" He scrutinized her like a recalcitrant child. "Does this have something to do with the remains your plumber dug up?"

She told him about the Brewer's spruce cone the deputies uncovered and why she'd thought it was significant.

He squinted up at the tree then at the cones on the ground, the muscles in his jaw twitching. "And now?"

She shrugged. "I'm not sure what to think." She played out the final hole, sure of one thing—she'd never been so relieved to finish a game.

"Join me for dinner?" Ted asked as he drove them to the clubhouse.

"Um . . ." Kaylee still couldn't quite fathom that Congressman

Munk was interested in her romantically. She was flattered, but her life was here now. Not in Washington, D.C., or the governor's mansion. Not to mention, he had to be a dozen years her senior. Although admittedly, he wore his age well.

"I'm going to take that as a no," he said, amusement coloring his tone.

She offered him a sheepish smile. "My garden club meets tonight. My friends are expecting me."

"Of course. Perhaps some other time," he said, although his tone suggested he knew it was unlikely. "Give me a minute to change, and I'll drive you back to the shop."

While waiting for Ted, Kaylee wandered up the hall to the lobby to see if Neil and his crew were still working. Now that the Brewer's spruce cone clue was a bust, she had no concrete evidence to connect a suspect to Danny's makeshift grave, but she still couldn't let the investigation drop. She could still hear her grandmother's worry. Kaylee needed answers, and she was certain that someone on this island had them. Maybe that someone was Neil.

"Hello there," a male voice said behind her. "Are you new here?"

Kaylee spun around. "No, just a guest."

The man was tall and lanky. His hair stuck to his head in the shape of a golf cap and he seemed to have spent some time in the lounge since finishing his round. He wagged a finger at her. "I know you. You're that florist that found Danny's body in her backyard."

She tilted her head. "Did you know Danny?"

"Sure. We went to school together." He shook his head. "It's unbelievable."

"You don't think Danny would've been prowling around the shop planning to rob it?" she asked.

"Oh yeah, wouldn't put that past him. The day before he disappeared he told me he was gonna come into a lot of money."

"From robbing the flower shop?" How would she tell her grandmother?

"He didn't say where he was getting it. Made it sound more like someone was just going to give it to him. Like he inherited it or something. When he didn't show up at school again, I figured he'd robbed someone and disappeared with the take. He always wanted to try to find his mom."

"It sounds as if the two of you were pretty close."

The guy shrugged, his gaze shifting to the window.

Outside, Neil was squatting in the garden six feet away, staring at them. His gaze collided with hers, and he abruptly gathered his tools and pushed to his feet.

"We sat in the cafeteria together at lunch," the guy beside her continued. "We weren't jocks. You know how high school kids are."

"Yeah," Kaylee said, wondering what had prompted Neil's quick exit. Something this guy knew?

Her pulse quickened as she returned her attention to the man beside her. "Did Danny ever talk about taking boats out for a spin?"

The guy tilted his head and peered at her through bleary eyes. "What you're really asking is if he killed that girl."

"There you are, Kaylee!" Ted strode toward them and swept an arm around her at the same time he pushed open the front door.

"Wait," she turned back to the man, but he was already tottering off toward the men's room.

Ted glanced over his shoulder. "I'm sorry you were subjected to that. Dwayne has a bad habit of hitting on women when he's had too much to drink." Ted thumbed a message into his phone, then collected Kaylee's golf bag outside the door and steered her toward the parking lot.

Neil chose that moment to speed off in a souped-up truck.

Ted snorted. "I see Digger still likes his transportation fast."

"And you don't?" Kaylee looked pointedly at the convertible.

"Touché."

"Mr. Spiece mentioned Neil used to race boats. Do you know anything about that?"

Ted loaded her borrowed clubs into his trunk and opened the passenger door for Kaylee. "Oh yeah. He was my prime competitor."

She chuckled. "I should've seen that one coming. Is there anything you don't compete in?"

"What can I say?" he said with a dramatic wave of his arm as he rounded the car and climbed in himself. "I enjoy a good contest."

"Does Neil still race boats?"

Ted glanced across the seat at her. "Who else did you ask about Joelle and Danny?"

"Pardon me?"

"All these questions." He started the car and backed out of his parking spot. "I'm beginning to see why someone might've sent you that note."

Her heart thumped. "How do you figure?"

"There are rumors Joelle and Digger had a fight the night she died. It would explain why she was alone in the boat. And why Neil was testy."

"Because he blames himself for not being there for her?"

Ted shrugged. "She'd probably still be alive if he had been."

Kaylee leaned back and chewed over that for a minute. "Do you think Neil would've taken the law into his own hands and gone after Danny?"

Ted glanced at her again, his gaze censuring. "Those kind

of inflammatory questions are how you start rumors that ruin an innocent person's reputation."

Or enrage a guilty person. Kaylee frowned. As a congressman, Ted likely had an unwelcome personal experience with such rumors. "I'm not trying to vilify Neil. I'm just looking for the truth." If Neil killed Danny to avenge Joelle's death, it would explain why neither he nor her father had bugged the sheriff's department for updates on the hunt for him after his disappearance.

Ted rubbed his five-o'clock shadow. "Well, I don't know what Digger might've been capable of. I suppose guilt can make people do crazy things."

Said like a true politician.

As they reached the edge of town, Kaylee spotted Neil's truck parked in front of Mr. Spiece's place. The man had mentioned that Neil took care of his yard. Did he take care of other things for the aging man too?

Joelle's dad could have informed Neil of Kaylee's visit and could have described her car to him. It was entirely possible for Neil to detour from his planned hiking trip to flatten her tires and leave her that note.

Guilt wasn't the only thing that made people do crazy things. Anger did too. Like maybe anger at her for stirring up old memories, possibly old crimes.

9

From the surprising number of cars outside the Old Cape Lighthouse keeper's quarters, Kaylee guessed that she was the last to arrive to the Petal Pushers garden club meeting—and that they had some guests. She'd asked Ted to drop her off to save time, since the lighthouse was closer to the country club than her shop. Someone must have heard Ted's Mustang pull up because by the time Ted hefted her borrowed bag of clubs out of the trunk, half a dozen faces were peeking out the front window.

"Thanks for the game," she said to Ted as he opened her door and she climbed out. "And for convincing Mrs. Banks to keep me as her florist."

"Not a problem. Take care." He got back into the driver's seat, then leaned across to the open passenger's side window where Kaylee still stood. "And don't forget I'd appreciate your vote."

Kaylee saluted. "You've got it."

As Ted sped off, she took a moment to soak in the ocean view and inhale the soothing sea air. Her rampant speculation at the sight of Neil's truck outside Walter Spiece's place on the drive over had left her more than a little rattled, but the warm orange glow of the setting sun soon restored her to an even keel.

Fevered whispering greeted her as she stepped inside the building.

"I didn't know you and the congressman were dating," Kathy said.

Befuddled by both the librarian's presence and her question, Kaylee stuttered, "We're not."

"Too bad," Kathy said. "He'd be a catch. Handsome. Athletic. He was the star quarterback on the high school team his senior year."

"He was the *starting* QB, not the star," Mary's husband, Herb, said with an eye roll. "And that was only because his dad bought the team new jerseys."

Kaylee raised an eyebrow at Jessica in an unspoken question about their extra members that evening.

"They figured we'd be discussing the mystery, not gardening," Jessica whispered.

"Amazing what greasing the right palms can get you," Jessica's husband, Luke, said in response to Herb's comment.

"What are you implying?" Kathy asked. "The congressman has a stellar public record."

"All right," Kaylee said brightly, not wanting the meeting to degrade into bickering over Ted's politics. "We're here to talk about plants, not Ted Munk."

"First, tell us what you learned about Danny. Mary said Eddie closed the investigation already." Jessica handed Kaylee a mug of coffee and a pastry from her shop. More treats were arranged on a platter on a nearby table.

Kaylee shared her grandmother's position that Danny was the victim of foul play and there was no way he drove the boat that hit Joelle's. She told them about how Ted's father had caught Danny attempting to take one of their boats. She also mentioned her conversation with Joelle's dad and Neil's cool reception outside the golf club. "The worst part is that the one clue I thought might break the case is a bust."

"What's that?" Jessica asked.

Kaylee told her about the *Picea breweriana* tree growing next to the golf course. "So Danny could've picked up the cone at any time and stuffed it in his pocket. All this time, I'd been thinking it must've dropped into the folds of his jacket off someone else, someone who'd vacationed in the Klamath Mountains."

"I might have a clue," DeeDee chimed in. "Mr. Barnes is one of my regular customers."

"Ooh, let me guess," Mary said. "He loves nautical mysteries." Mr. Barnes owned the island's oldest boat-building and repair business.

DeeDee shook her head. "You'd think so, but art crime mysteries are his favorite. Anyway, he told me that after Joelle's accident, he scrutinized all the boats that came to him for repairs for a possible connection, but never found any."

"We already knew that," Kathy said.

"Yes, but because of that, the police concluded the perpetrator scuttled the boat."

"So?" Kathy raised her eyebrows.

"So, if Danny stole the boat that caused the accident, as people claimed, you'd think the boat's owner would've come forward and reported the theft, but no one ever did. And we know there's no way he owned a boat." DeeDee reached for a cookie.

Straightening, Kaylee set down her untouched coffee. "You might be on to something."

"The theft victim might've been afraid the police would think he was guilty if he came forward," Mary said. "Especially if the police later found the boat, but failed to find Danny's fingerprints on it."

Jessica's eyes widened. "Maybe someone found damage on his boat and feared one of his children caused the damage, and possibly caused the accident, and he covered it up for their protection."

Kaylee sighed. "We have too many theories and no proof of anything. And in the meantime, Grandma is beating herself up for not doing more to protect Danny."

Mary patted her hand. "No one did more for that boy than Bea, and everyone knows it."

"You know, the farm next to the golf course used to belong to the Spieces," Herb said.

Kaylee did a double take. "I had no idea." Why hadn't Ted told her? He must've known. Then again, he probably hadn't wanted to give her another reason to irritate the note writer.

"Walter Spiece could've lashed out at Danny, believing Danny caused his daughter's accident," Jessica said.

"But why would Danny have visited the Spiece farm?" Mary asked.

"Maybe Danny went to set the record straight about the rumors floating around about him," Kaylee said. Even as she said it, though, she knew it was a stretch.

The discussion finally turned to gardening, but Kaylee found it impossible to keep her thoughts from straying to the case. Was she crazy to think she could find evidence linking someone to a thirty-five-year-old homicide?

"Would you like a lift back to the shop for your car?" Mary asked her as the meeting broke up for the night, and Kaylee carried the bag of golf clubs she had borrowed to Mary's vehicle.

"No thanks. It's a nice evening. I'd like to walk."

A worried look flitted across Mary's face. "Until we figure out who sent you that creepy note, I don't think it's a good idea for you to be out walking alone after dark."

Kaylee wanted to argue. She hated the idea of caving in to the scare tactic, but practicality prevailed. "Well, I'm sure Bear would appreciate my getting home sooner," she said. She had enlisted Bridget Joplin, the neighbor girl, to play with Bear for a while outside after school, but that had been hours ago. Kaylee climbed into the back of Mary and Herb's car.

As Herb pulled the car up in front of The Flower Patch,

Mr. Fitzpatrick, who lived above his shop on the street behind, rounded the corner with his dog. "Evening, Miss Bleu," he said.

Kaylee waved goodbye to Mary and Herb, then petted the man's small poodle and asked after his family.

"Oh, the missus has rheumatism and it's acting up. She says rain is coming, which means Reese got your well covered just in time."

"You talked to him?"

"Nah. We can see your yard from our kitchen window. I remember one time I couldn't sleep and went out to the kitchen for a glass of milk and spotted a prowler back there."

Kaylee's pulse quickened. "Recently?"

"There, there." He must've heard the concern in her voice, because he patted her shoulder comfortingly. "It was years ago. When my son was still in school."

Kaylee relaxed at that. "What did you do?"

"Shouted out to him that I was calling the sheriff."

"Did you?"

Mr. Fitzpatrick chuckled. "No, the guy took off like a shot. I heard his vehicle door slam and tires squeal away. I figured the sheriff would never find him and headed back to bed."

"Well, it's nice to know I have a neighbor keeping an eye on the place," Kaylee said with a smile.

"That's what we do here." Mr. Fizpatrick waved and began to make his way down the street again.

But his description brought to mind the way Neil had sped off from the golf club earlier this evening. "Mr. Fitzpatrick," she called after him. "Do you happen to remember when you saw the prowler in the shop's yard?"

He stared skyward, scratching his whiskers. "You know, normally, there'd be no way. But that was a weekend etched in just about everyone's minds around here. It was the Monday—no, the Sunday night after my son's classmate was killed in a boating accident."

"Joelle Spiece?" Kaylee scarcely managed to breathe the name aloud.

"That's right."

Kaylee's heart jumped to her throat. "You're sure?"

"Sure I'm sure. Your grandmother had a hole in the yard then too. George was just putting in the new well."

His eyes widened. "Oh." He gasped, clearly making the possible connection to the remains the police had been investigating.

"Did you see the vehicle? Was it a car? A truck?"

"I didn't see it, but come to think of it, the engine did make a racket. More like a truck."

"We need to call the sheriff," Kaylee said.

Mr. Fitzpatrick and his poodle waited with Kaylee for the sheriff in her shop.

"Bear is going to have his nose out of joint when he smells you on me," she said to the friendly poodle. She glanced at the messages Mary had taken in her absence—three of them from Mrs. Banks with additional requests for Chelsea's reception. Kaylee tucked them into her job folder, then peeked out the front window. "The sheriff should be here any minute."

A pickup truck was parked across the street, one store down, and a flicker of light inside it made her suspect someone sat inside. Was someone watching her store? Was it Neil?

It was too dark to tell if his company's logo was emblazoned on the door. All the nearby stores, like hers, were already closed, so the driver couldn't be waiting for someone shopping or finishing their shift.

She stared at the truck's window, but didn't see the light again and couldn't detect any movement inside. Maybe she'd been mistaken.

A moment later, Eddie Maddox pulled up in front of the shop. By the time Kaylee got to the front door and opened it, the pickup truck had taken off. *Okay, that's creepy.* Maybe whoever it was saw the sheriff's vehicle and took off. But what honest citizen would want to avoid law enforcement?

"I'm afraid we need to make this quick," the sheriff said without preamble. "Another call came in on my way over here. Deputy Brooks is going straight there, but he'll likely need assistance."

Mr. Fitzpatrick quickly repeated his story about the prowler for the sheriff.

"You're certain about the date?" Maddox asked.

"Yes sir."

"So Danny couldn't have been alone in the yard," Kaylee said. "Because Mr. Fitzpatrick saw someone take off in what he thinks was a truck. And that someone probably pushed Danny into the hole and left him for dead, if he wasn't already."

"You're making some big assumptions there," the sheriff said, closing his notepad. "We have no way of knowing this occurred the same night Danny went into the hole, let alone the same time."

"George worked on the well on that Saturday and the hole was refilled Monday morning," Mr. Fitzpatrick said. "I remember because I'd been talking over the fence with George about that poor girl's death. And George doesn't work on Sundays."

The sheriff nodded.

"Don't you think it raises enough doubt to reopen the investigation into Danny's death?" Kaylee asked.

Maddox scraped his jaw contemplatively. "After thirty-five years, there's little chance of identifying the vehicle Fitzpatrick heard speed off, let alone its driver. For all we know, it was Danny he spooked and that's what landed him in the hole. The sound of the vehicle speeding off could have been unrelated."

Kaylee turned to Mr. Fitzpatrick, who was starting to look every one of his eighty years and then some. "Did you see the prowler leave the yard and climb into a vehicle?"

He shook his head. "It was too dark. I saw a flash of movement. Then I heard the door slam, the engine roar to life, and the tires squeal."

The sheriff gave Kaylee an "I rest my case" expression.

She shook her head. "But then who's sending me—"

An urgent summons from dispatch over Maddox's radio cut short Kaylee's spiel on the cryptic note she had received.

"10-66," the sheriff barked into his radio. "On my way." Rushing toward the door, he said over his shoulder to Kaylee, "Sorry, I've got to go. We'll talk about this later."

As the door slammed behind him, Kaylee turned to Mr. Fitzpatrick. "Any idea what a 10-66 is?"

He shook his head.

She pulled out her phone and tapped in a search of police codes. "Here it is." Her heart fell. "No wonder he was in such a hurry."

"What is it?" Mr. Fitzpatrick asked.

"Notify medical examiner." Someone was dead.

10

"What do you say we ride the bike to the shop today?" Kaylee said to Bear as she tied a bright red bow tie around his neck. She'd slept poorly again thanks to bad dreams, uneasiness about the sheriff's urgent call, and high winds whistling through the cottage's eaves. She hoped the tie's jaunty color would help energize her. "I need a good workout to sweep the cobwebs from my head."

Bear yipped his approval of the proposal.

"It's settled then. We need to get in our bike rides while we still can." With the days getting shorter, it would soon be dark by the time she closed the shop at night. She scooped up her little dachshund and locked the cottage. She set Bear in the carrier basket on her handlebars. "Comfy?"

Bear let out another yip and panted, his tongue lolling out as if he were smiling. He did love their bike rides.

The salty ocean breeze transported her to bygone days of building sandcastles on the beach and racing her brother down the sand dunes. Her reminiscing evaporated when she rounded a bend and spotted a couple of Neil Dykstra's landscaping trucks. Her suddenly racing heart had nothing to do with the hill she was pedaling up. Images of Mr. Fitzpatrick's tire-squealing prowler racing from the shop's yard had replayed in her mind most of the night, and an irrational, throw-caution-to-the-wind part of her wanted to see Neil's reaction to the story.

Sure, he wasn't the only tire squealer on the island by far, but he was the only one she knew who also had a reason to despise Danny.

Neil's crew was laying a flagstone path, but Neil didn't appear to be among them. "Looking good," she said, as she approached the yard.

Randy flashed her a toothy grin. "It better be. We've put enough work into it."

"Your boss not with you today?" she asked.

"Nope," Bob said, reaching into the back of the truck for another flagstone.

From the corner of her eye, Kaylee glimpsed him give Randy a silencing glare.

Why so secretive? She stopped her bike and lowered a foot to the ground to hold herself steady. "Do you know where I can find him?" When no one answered, she stared at each crewman in turn until each met her gaze and acknowledged her question with a shake of the head. "No one knows where he is?" She found that hard to believe. It was more likely they were being protective of his privacy.

Bob brushed by her bike and Bear let out a growl.

Randy leaned toward Kaylee and spoke in a low voice. "Digger had business off-island today, but you didn't hear it from me." He straightened quickly as Bob headed back their way.

Interesting. Had her probing into Danny's history prompted Neil's sudden departure?

For the rest of the bike ride, Kaylee theorized reasons for Neil's off-island business. He could merely be visiting his suppliers, but then why wouldn't his employees say so? Randy made it sound as if Neil, or at least Bob, wouldn't want her to know the reason for his excursion.

Kaylee held out her arm to signal her turn into Death by Chocolate for her morning coffee.

A car horn blared.

Kaylee swerved toward the ditch and screeched to a stop,

barely staying upright. Bear gave a startled yip and pressed himself into the basket.

Brakes screeched and a huffing woman slammed her car door. "Watch where you're going!"

Recognizing the strident voice of Mrs. Banks without having to look, Kaylee silently counted to ten as she straightened her bike.

"Oh it's you," Mrs. Banks said. She faced Kaylee, planting her fisted hands on her hips. "Did you get my messages about the changes to the flower order?"

Kaylee pasted on a smile. *I'm fine. Thank you for asking.* Aloud, she said, "Yes I did. We can accommodate your preferences with no problem."

"We'll go with the brass candlesticks you showed us. And I think we'd prefer aquamarine rather than turquoise for the main color."

Kaylee nodded.

"And absolutely no lilies. My sister can't tolerate the fragrance." Mrs. Banks paused and gave Kaylee the once-over. "Shouldn't you be writing this down?"

Uh, I'm standing on the side of the road with my bike. "Candlesticks. Aqua. No lilies," she said. "I won't forget."

"See that you don't." Mrs. Banks wagged her finger. "You wouldn't want a bad report getting back to Congressman Munk."

Mrs. Banks sped off, revealing Ted's assistant standing outside the coffee shop. She gave Kaylee an empathetic smile.

"You heard that, huh?" Kaylee grimaced.

"Hmm. Sounds as if the congressman's good word on your behalf may not have been so great a favor after all."

Kaylee walked her bike across the road. "Nah, it'll be fine. She just wants everything to be perfect for her daughter's wedding. I've dealt with that before."

Raylene's eyebrows lifted ever so slightly. "She's fortunate to have such an understanding florist." And with that, she headed off toward the harbor carrying a takeout tray of coffees.

"You wait here, Bear," Kaylee said as she approached the coffee shop door. "I'll only be a minute, and then we'll walk down to the harbor."

Bear let out an approving woof.

The door opened, held by Reese. He gave Kaylee a smile. "I was hoping to catch you before I left."

"Oh?"

He motioned to Jessica behind the counter, who held up a book. "I was retrofitting bookcases at the high school library yesterday and spotted their archive of yearbooks. They let me borrow the yearbook for Danny and Joelle's last year. I thought it might help you find old friends of theirs who might know something."

"Great idea." Kaylee felt her mood lifting. "Thank you."

Reese reclaimed the book from Jessica, who shot Kaylee an impish smile.

"I'll take my usual," Kaylee said to her, ignoring the innuendo behind her grin.

As Reese took a seat at a nearby table, Jessica whispered, "The man was thinking about you while working. Doesn't that tell you something?"

"Yes, he enjoys solving a good mystery as much as the rest of us."

Jessica shook her head. "You're so deluded. If he weren't seven years younger than me and I wasn't already married, you wouldn't catch me letting the grass grow under my feet." She touched a flower on the lavender geranium that graced her counter. "Oliver is portending a good day."

Keith Phelps, the clerk from the computer store, chuckled at Jessica's superstitious prediction from beside Kaylee at the counter.

Kaylee paid for her coffee and turned to Reese's table. She

didn't doubt he was the most handsome bachelor on the island, with those sky-blue eyes and that disarming smile. But that didn't make Jessica's implications true.

He stopped leafing through the yearbook and pointed to a student photo. "This is Danny."

Kaylee scrutinized the photo, thinking his face was familiar. She glanced at a group of teens crowded around the table next to theirs, dangerously close to being late for their morning classes. "Ever notice how students in old yearbooks always look older than current students?"

"I think it's because the hairstyles and clothes are old."

"You might be right."

Reese leafed through more pages. "It doesn't appear that Danny was involved in any athletics or clubs, but Joelle was on the cheerleading squad and on the yearbook committee." Reese stopped at a page filled with photographs of different school teams and oriented it so Kaylee could see it better. "Her boyfriend was on the football team, the track-and-field team, and the boating team."

"As was Ted Munk, I see."

"Yeah." Reese's tone soured. Maybe he wasn't big on politics, or just didn't agree with Ted on such matters. "He was a popular subject of the candid shots too." Reese turned to a page near the back of the book. "They did a nice 'In Memoriam' page for Joelle."

Kaylee pulled it close to examine. "May I hang onto this for a day or two?" Perhaps one of the candid snapshots would reveal something they were missing.

He grinned at her eagerness. "You really enjoy moonlighting as a detective."

She ducked her head. "I've gained a fair bit of experience at it over the years."

He tapped the yearbook. "Well, Detective Bleu, you can

have it for two weeks." He gathered his jacket from the back of his chair. "I have to get going. Let me know if you need a hand with anything else."

"I'll do that. Thank you." She scooped up the yearbook and her coffee to enjoy with Bear along the ocean.

Outside, Bear waited patiently.

"Sorry for making you wait, buddy." She showed him the yearbook. "But this might give us the breakthrough we need." She tucked it under her arm and walked the dachshund down to the harbor.

Ted waved to her from a fancy boat. "Would you like to join us on our fishing trip?" he called.

"Sorry, I can't. I have to be at the shop. But thanks for asking."

He waved an acknowledgment and untied the boat as Raylene climbed off. She ambled down the dock and grazed Kaylee's arm as she passed, almost spilling Kaylee's coffee.

"Oh, so sorry about that," Raylene said, stopping.

"Not into fishing?" Kaylee asked her.

"I've got bigger fish to fry." A conspiratorial twinkle winked in her eye as she gestured to the laptop bag she carried. "Duty calls."

Kaylee chuckled. Raylene clearly took her job seriously, despite never seeming quite happy.

Kaylee strolled with Bear along the pebbled shoreline, sipping her coffee and drinking in the tranquil sound of the lapping water. Bear attempted to paw a crab that scuttled sideways away from him.

"One of these days, one of those guys is going to snap back at you. Then you'll think twice about trying to touch them."

Bear ignored her. Kaylee swirled the coffee still in her cup and scrutinized the surface. It seemed fine, but for some reason it tasted off this morning, as if her cup hadn't been properly rinsed free of dish soap—except that it was a disposable cup. She took one last sip and chucked the half-empty cup in a trash can.

Checking the time on her phone, Kaylee gave Bear's lead a gentle tug. "C'mon, we need to open the shop."

Mary arrived at the same time as Kaylee and flipped the shop's sign to *Open*. "I think I'll spruce up our window displays this morning. I noticed some of the plants weren't looking so good."

Kaylee rubbed her queasy stomach, suddenly not feeling so well herself. "I hope it's not a problem with the water. I'd better have it tested." She set the yearbook on the counter and unlatched Bear's lead.

"I doubt it," Mary said. "Only the plants by this window seem to be struggling."

Kaylee examined the leaves for signs of a fungus or virus and noticed an odd-colored residue on the soil in some of the pots. "Did you fertilize these recently?"

Mary shook her head. "That's your department."

Kaylee studied the residue more closely, wishing she had a microscope to confirm her suspicion. "These plants can't tolerate acidic soil, and it looks as if they've been spiked with sulfur, which causes that."

The bell above the door jangled as customers who'd meandered up from the ferry dock entered.

"Could you take care of the customers?" Kaylee asked. "I need to repot these." She carried the plants to the workroom and filled new pots with fresh soil. Could the switch to Jessica's water while the shop's was out of commission have caused this? There'd sure been an odd taste in the coffee this morning. She should alert Jessica that she might want to test her water.

Another wave of nausea roiled Kaylee's stomach. She snatched up her phone and called Death by Chocolate. "Hey Jess, when's the last time you had your water tested?"

"I actually got the latest test results back this morning. We got a perfect score. Why? Yours testing bad?"

"No, but I noticed an odd taste in this morning's coffee."

"Oh dear. I'm sorry. I don't know what that could be. I didn't change anything, and I haven't had any other complaints."

"When I got to the shop, we noticed that some of the plants we'd watered with your water look as if they've gotten too much acidity in their soil."

"Hold on a second."

Kaylee could hear the sound of a tap running on the other end of the phone and took the opportunity to grab a couple of crackers from the cupboard to help settle her stomach.

Jessica came back on the line. "The water tastes normal to me and to Gretchen." She spoke quietly. "Maybe your note writer spiked your coffee?" Jessica sucked in a loud breath. "Glen Phelps's son Keith was in here when you were, wasn't he?"

Kaylee stifled a hiccup, sorry she'd set off Jessica's speculating. "My constitution's probably just off this morning, which could've made the coffee taste weird to me."

"If you start feeling any worse, make sure you get to the doctor right away."

"I will."

"By the way, I didn't get the chance to ask you this morning: What did the sheriff say about the note?"

"I haven't had a chance to show it to him yet."

"Still?" Jessica's voice kicked up an octave. "Kaylee, you need to do that."

"I will. I promise."

"Kaylee?" Mary called from the front of the store.

"I've got to go," Kaylee said to Jessica. "Mary needs me out front." Kaylee hurried out, but the shop was empty.

"There's something here you need to see," Mary said from behind the computer monitor.

Bear whined at the odd note in Mary's tone.

"What is it?"

"A car crash."

Kaylee rushed to her side. "Someone we know? Were they badly hurt?"

At the sight of the bold, blood-red message scrawled across the screen, Kaylee's blood ran cold.

THIS IS WHAT HAPPENS TO PEOPLE WHO DON'T HEED WARNINGS.

11

"Who sent this?" Kaylee demanded. She squinted past the ugly message on the computer screen to examine the news article. Beneath an image of a crumpled car rammed against a tree was the caption *Impaired driver loses life.*

Mary scrolled to the top of the message. "Yourfault@qmail.com. This is just sick."

"You think the sender is the same person who sent the cut-and-paste note?"

"Don't you?"

"It could be a mass e-mail sent out as a wake-up call by a mother against drunk driving. Way too many people still drink and drive. Just yesterday at the country club . . ." Kaylee's thoughts flashed to the inebriated man she'd been talking to about Danny. "Where'd the car in the picture crash? Do they identify the driver?"

Mary scrolled down and hovered over the hyperlink to the story. "It's not usually a good idea to click on links in anonymous e-mails."

"No, you're right. Go on the Internet and do a search on the crash."

Mary found what they wanted on a local news website. "The victim was Dwayne Matthews, 51. He lost control of his car on his way home from the country club. Alcohol was a factor. No one else was involved."

Kaylee's heart hammered in her chest. *Could it be the same guy?* Ted had mentioned his name, but she couldn't remember it. "Search for a picture of the victim."

Mary typed his name into the search engine and a photo of the man appeared on the screen.

Kaylee's mouth went dry. "I talked to that guy about Danny Lane. He knew him from high school. He said Danny bragged about coming into money. I'd just asked him if Danny ever bragged about taking boats out for a joyride when Ted hurried me away because he thought the guy was trying to hit on me."

"Was he?"

"I don't know. Maybe, but not very well." Kaylee stared at his image on the screen. "I think he could've told me more about Danny."

"Do you think your note writer killed him because he knew too much?"

Kaylee shivered at the horrific suggestion. "It was a single-vehicle crash." Everything in her recoiled at the idea the man was killed because she had talked to him. "There's no mention of foul play, right? So worst-case scenario, the sender saw this morning's news photo as a sickeningly graphic way to shock me into heeding his earlier warning."

Mary frowned. "But this isn't a random accident the sender plucked out of the daily news. You talked to the victim. Just yesterday. About Danny. Don't you think that's a little too coincidental?"

Kaylee squirmed. *Yeah. Way too coincidental.*

"Who saw you talking to this Dwayne guy?" Mary asked.

"Ted. Besides him, I suppose anyone could've passed by in the hall without me noticing." She stared out the window without really seeing anything as she tried to recall. "Neil! He saw us through the window. His crew too, I imagine."

Mary picked up the phone and started dialing.

"Who are you calling?"

"The sheriff's department. They should be able to figure out who really sent this e-mail."

"Sheriff Maddox won't be happy to learn I'm poking around asking questions about Danny."

Mary brushed off the protest with a swish of her hand. "He can be unhappy with you all he wants. As far as I'm concerned, this proves you're on to something."

Eddie Maddox arrived an hour later with a computer expert he said would be able to trace the sender's IP address. "We might not be able to connect the e-mail address to a person, since anyone can lie about who they are when they set one up, but we should be able to pinpoint where it came from."

The very young consultant sat down behind the computer and tapped keys in rapid-fire succession.

"Where'd you find this guy?" Mary asked. "He doesn't look old enough to be out of high school."

"He isn't," Maddox said. "He's my neighbor's son. A total genius on the computer."

Thankfully Kaylee's stomach had settled, and her spirits lifted as she watched the youth in action. If her harasser turned out to have any connection to Danny's death, he was going to be sorry he tried to spook her out of asking questions.

As the teen worked on the computer and Mary went to build a birthday bouquet, Kaylee filled the sheriff in on the other note and the flat-tire incident, as well as her conversation with Dwayne and the fact Neil had been at the country club and had likely seen her talking to him.

"We found no evidence anyone or anything but Dwayne driving while intoxicated had anything to do with the accident. Can you think of any other reason this person might be warning you to mind your own business?" he asked.

"None that I can think of. I forgot to mention that Neil Dykstra suddenly went off-island today and his employees were very cagey with me about why."

"Neil is free to come and go as he pleases. I doubt a trip off-island is unusual for him. And his employees are not obligated to inform you of his whereabouts."

"You're sure no one sabotaged Dwayne Matthews's car, or otherwise helped it off the road?"

"The man's blood alcohol level was twice the legal limit. Trust me, he didn't need any help. He already had two previous DUI citations too."

"At least he alone paid for his irresponsibility," Mary interjected. "It would have been awful if he'd injured anyone else."

"Well, I can tell you one thing about your pen pal," the young man behind the computer said. "He's computer savvy. Or has a friend who is."

"You can't track the IP address?" Maddox asked.

"Nope. Can't even narrow it down to a region. He used every trick in the book."

The sheriff rubbed his forehead. "What can you tell us about him? Anything?"

The teen shrugged. "He's probably on a VPN."

"What's that?"

"A virtual private network. Big corporations use them to protect their data. It works like a private encrypted tunnel into the Internet, allowing the user to create a secure connection to another network. He's also probably not on a PC. They're pretty easy to hack."

Kaylee cringed at the thought of this guy not only sending her creepy e-mails, but actually hacking into her computer system and wreaking who knew what kind of havoc on her business records.

"And he used an anonymous e-mailer," the teen continued. "That was the easiest part. Although some guys will use a legit e-mail account and exploit remailers to hide the origin. I can't tell which this guy did."

"Who on the island would have the know-how to do something like this?" Kaylee asked.

The boy grinned. "Half the guys in my computer class."

"Are you serious?"

He shrugged. "Anyone could do an Internet search and figure it out."

"But that news article was only posted an hour before the e-mail was sent," Eddie pointed out. "Could someone figure out how to hide their identity that quickly?"

"Not with confidence. More likely he already knew or enlisted someone to send it for him."

"Or her," Mary said. "They say cut-and-paste notes are usually the work of a woman." Apparently Mary had been reading the same mysteries as DeeDee.

"I don't know anything about that," the teen said. "But all the computer geeks I know are guys."

The sheriff thanked him for his help. To Kaylee he said, "Let me know if you receive anything else or see anyone suspicious."

"So are you going to reopen the investigation into Danny's death?" Kaylee asked.

"I'm far from convinced your note writer is his killer. Why would he stir the pot when I've already closed the investigation?"

"Maybe he didn't know you had. Or maybe he's worried I might turn up something that would make you change your mind."

"Something more than a threatening note?" Sheriff Maddox tucked his notebook in his shirt pocket and headed for the door. "I suspect it'll be someone who doesn't appreciate you upsetting a lot of people by asking questions. And just in case he or she intends to act on the warning if you don't listen, I'd suggest you keep a low profile."

Kaylee pressed her lips together against her protest. She wanted to know the truth, but telling Maddox so would only invite a lecture. She thanked him for his time and watched him leave. "What do you think?" she asked Mary as the door closed behind him.

Mary's gaze drifted to the front window. "There's only two people I can think of who could pull off hiding their IP address."

"I'm guessing Neil and Mr. Spiece aren't them," Kaylee said.

"No, but either man could've gotten help. In fact, one of them is a good friend of Mr. Spiece's. And had no love lost for Danny."

"Glen Phelps," Kaylee said.

"Or his son Keith."

Kaylee grabbed her coat. "I think I'll pay our local computer store a visit. You okay with watching the shop?"

"Of course."

The bell of the store rang and Bear let out an echoing yip as DeeDee's husband, Andy, and their two girls came in. Polly and Zoe skipped over to Bear and made a much-appreciated fuss over him. Andy set a box of DeeDee's handcrafted soap on the counter. "DeeDee said you were sold out of her soap?"

"Wow, she got these done quickly," Mary said.

"They're from the display in her bookshop. For some reason, they sell much better from here."

Kaylee chuckled. "Her shoppers are probably too engrossed in the books to notice soap."

"Can we play with Bear in the yard?" the girls called, already jockeying toward the side door.

"If it's okay with your dad, Bear would love that."

"Sure," Andy said. "Just stay in the yard. I have a couple of errands to finish, and then I'll come back and pick you up."

Kaylee followed Andy out and walked the block and a half to Get Wired. Keith Phelps, a stout, balding man in his late fifties, was alone in the store, tapping away on a computer keyboard. "May I help you?" he asked with a quick tap of a button that blackened his screen.

His complexion was a splotchy red, but Kaylee couldn't be sure if it was a reaction to almost being caught at whatever he'd been doing or simply his normal color.

"I hope so." She held his gaze for a long, silent moment and decided to go for the direct approach. "Did you e-mail my shop this morning?"

Half a dozen micro-expressions flitted across his face so quickly that she was at a loss how to interpret them. "No, sorry. Why? Did your reply bounce?"

"I didn't reply. Is your dad around?"

"Afraid not. Did you bring your computer with you?" He cleared a spot on the counter. "Because if you're having trouble sending replies to your e-mails—"

"That's not my problem." She opted to try a different tactic. "I don't want the recipient to be able to trace my IP address and ID me or figure out where I am."

"Right. Totally understand. A lot of people are getting uncomfortable with the way browsers track your online habits these days. For a modest monthly fee, you could download a VPN and operate through that. I'd be happy to help you choose the one that's right for you."

Two more customers came into the store and Keith asked her to excuse him a moment, then moved on to them.

When he finally returned to her, Kaylee said, "Could you just send an e-mail for me? Making it anonymous I mean. Have you ever done that?"

"Well, we use a VPN, so theoretically, yes, all my e-mails have their IP address masked, but the recipient would see my e-mail address."

"But you can hide that too, right?"

"Sure, I suppose, but why would you want to? You do know that it's against the law to spam a bunch of e-mail addresses to advertise your business, right? People have to sign up to get e-mails from you."

Kaylee suddenly had the feeling she was being watched, but the other customers had already vacated the store. She checked the ceiling for video surveillance cameras, thinking Glen Phelps could be watching from a back room. The only such cameras were the ones the shop had for sale, including the demo model that brought her image up on an accompanying monitor beside it on the shelf. "Oh I know. But have you ever done it? Verified that the sender couldn't be traced?"

"No." His gaze shifted to a point past her right shoulder. "I've never had a reason to be concerned about it."

She tracked his gaze to the plate glass window at the front of the store, resisting the sudden urge to duck, as if someone were standing outside with a loaded rifle or something. No one was there.

Oh boy. My imagination is getting seriously out of control.

"And no one else has asked you to send an e-mail for them in the last 24 hours?" she pressed.

Keith cocked his head. "I don't want to sound rude, but if someone had, I doubt they'd appreciate me discussing the fact with other customers."

"You're right, of course." And that sure sounded like an affirmative answer to her. She turned her attention to the video monitoring system. "I'm thinking of installing one of these in my shop. How long does it record before you have to record over other days?"

"Seventy-two hours."

"Wow, that's impressive. And if, say, I want to look back on footage from earlier in the day, how would I do that?" She held her breath, praying he would demonstrate, so she could see who else visited his store this morning.

He did, then advanced the recording at five times the speed to the current time. She'd counted six people, not counting the two that had just left. Three customers had had their backs to the camera the entire time, but one seemed to be about the same size and stature as Mr. Spiece. Of the other three, Kaylee recognized only Keith's father—who clearly despised Danny. "I'll think it over. Thank you for your time."

Keith handed her a business card. "Happy to help."

As she turned toward the door, a flash of movement at the window made her bristle. She spun around. "You know what I would like to get today. A dash camera." If the creepy feeling she was being watched was justified, a dash cam might be just the gadget to help her catch the perp. "Do you sell those?"

"We sure do." He pulled one off the shelf behind the counter.

"Perfect. I'll take it."

A few minutes later, Keith had rung up her purchase and handed her a bag with her camera inside. As she stepped out of the shop, the engine on the black truck parked at the curb across the road started. She was pretty sure a similar truck had been parked outside the flower shop the previous night. Remembering that a black truck had also passed her when she'd stopped to talk to Neil's crew this morning, she made a mental note of the license plate.

When she returned to The Flower Patch, she peeked in the side yard and saw Polly and Zoe rolling around in the falling leaves with Bear. "Having fun?" she called.

They clambered to their feet and dashed over to the fence with Bear at their heels. "Bear is so much fun," Polly said.

"He's enjoying having playmates." The rumble of an engine diverted Kaylee's attention.

The same black truck pulled to the curb in front of her shop.

Kaylee turned to confront the driver, but Polly reached over the short fence and caught her by the arm. "Could you talk our Mom into letting us get a dog?" she asked pleadingly.

Kaylee pulled a stray leaf from the girl's hair. Though eight and the younger of the two, Polly was the spokesperson. "I'll see what I can do." She winked encouragingly.

The girls jumped up and down, cheering.

Mary poked her head outside to see what the commotion was about.

Andy sauntered up to the fence and paused next to Kaylee. "Something tells me I don't want to know what that cheer was about."

The girls spoke in overlapping, jumbled sentences about how much they wanted a dog.

Their dad opened the gate for them. "Look at you two. I think you're bringing half of Kaylee's yard with you." He plucked leaves and pine needles and even a pinecone out of the folds of their clothes and jacket pockets.

Kaylee gasped.

Fortunately, the three Wilcoxes were so busy negotiating the possibility of adding a dog to the family that they didn't notice.

"You okay?" Mary asked as the children skipped away with their dad.

Kaylee turned wide eyes to her. "I think I know where Danny Lane was killed."

12

"What? How?" Mary exclaimed, then shot a glance at passersby on the sidewalk and tugged Kaylee inside the flower shop. "Where do you think Danny was killed?"

"At Mr. Spiece's former property next to the golf course."

"Where you saw the spruce tree?"

"Exactly." Kaylee motioned toward the yard. "DeeDee's girls got all kinds of leaves and needles in their hair and clothes from rolling around with Bear. I'm thinking that either Danny had a tussle with Neil or Mr. Spiece in his yard before being killed in the shop's yard, or he was killed at the farm then dragged across the ground under the tree to a vehicle to dispose of the body here."

"Great theory, but how do we prove it?"

"I think I need to pay Mr. Spiece another visit. Let him know about the unique spruce cone buried with Danny's body. If he killed Danny or knows who did, I suspect he'll give himself away one way or another."

"I don't like the idea of you going there again. Not after that e-mail. Did Keith or Glen give you any leads in that department?"

"Not exactly. I didn't even see Glen. Keith wouldn't confirm or deny whether he sent an e-mail on someone's behalf, so I'm inclined to think he might have. I did get a glimpse at his store's surveillance recording though, and a guy who looked like Mr. Spiece from the back was there this morning."

Mary slapped the counter, making Bear jump two inches off the ground. "That settles it. You are not going to that man's house alone again. He could be waiting for you with a loaded shotgun."

"Actually"—Kaylee motioned Mary deeper into the store

and directed her attention to the black pickup truck parked out front. "I think that's the guy behind the e-mail."

Mary squinted at the truck's window. "Who is it?" she whispered, as if he might hear her.

"I don't know. He passed me when I was riding to work this morning. Then he trailed me up the street to the computer store and back. I think he was outside the shop last night. I was about to confront him when the girls distracted me."

"We've got to call the sheriff."

"No need," a female voice rang out from behind a display of vases. Deputy Dean Skenandore's wife, Joy, stepped into view. "Sorry for eavesdropping. I came in while you two were outside and when you returned your conversation seemed so intense, I didn't want to interrupt." She glanced at her cell phone and gave a satisfied nod at something she'd read. "I happened to be at the sheriff's office dropping off Dean's lunch when Eddie returned from checking out your nasty e-mail, so I already knew a little of what's been going on. I just texted Dean and told him he needs to get over here."

"Perfect," Kaylee said. "While the deputy is occupying the pickup driver with questions, I can sneak out the back and take the delivery van over to see Mr. Spiece."

Mary frowned. "I don't know."

Bear whined a protest as well.

"I do." Kaylee plucked a bouquet of carnations from the cooler and wrapped it. "I'll take this to him. That way, if anyone is watching me, it will look as if I'm simply making a delivery."

Five minutes later, Deputy Skenandore parked his cruiser behind the pickup truck, and Kaylee headed toward the shop's back door. "I won't be long."

Ten minutes later, she parked the shop van in Mr. Spiece's driveway. The curtains were drawn, and yet no lights appeared to be on inside. Her heart did a flip at the memory of Mary's fear that Mr. Spiece would be waiting for her with a loaded shotgun.

She glanced around the neighborhood and saw no sign of anyone watching her. She grabbed the bouquet of carnations and marched to the front door.

After she rang the doorbell and knocked several times, his neighbor happened up his side yard and said, "He's not home. Neil took him to visit his daughter."

"What time was that?"

"Seven this morning."

That was before Mr. Spiece's look-alike visited Get Wired. "Does his daughter live on the island?"

"Nope."

Well, that explained Neil's sudden off-island trip, but maybe not his true motivation. Did he want Mr. Spiece away from her? Or from the sheriff's probing?

"Any idea when he plans to be back?" Kaylee asked, with a wave of the bouquet so he'd think she wanted to know when to return with the delivery.

"He usually goes for a week at a time."

"Oh, I'd better not leave the flowers then. Thank you for letting me know." She turned back to her vehicle and, at the sight of Reese casually leaning against the van watching her, let out an embarrassing squeak.

How had she not heard him drive up? A shiver rippled through her at how easily someone with a ruthless agenda could've done the same. "What brings you here?" she asked, with a brightness that sounded fake, even to her own ears. By the maple-colored stains on his arms, he'd been in the middle of refinishing something.

"Mary called. She was worried about you."

Kaylee smiled. It was nice to know she had people watching

her back. She glanced up and down the street and saw no sign of Reese's truck. "How did you get here?"

"I'm building a deck for Ted Munk." He pointed between two houses further down the street to the yard of a massive estate set back from the road. "Mary told me about the e-mail."

Kaylee grimaced, waiting for a lecture.

Unlike Ted, however, Reese didn't try to talk her out of snooping. Instead, he said, "Next time you want to question a potential suspect, call me and I'll go with you. No point in taking unnecessary chances."

"I'll do that. Thanks." She opened the van's passenger door and set the carnation bouquet back on the seat.

"Did you learn anything useful?" Reese asked.

"Only that if Mr. Spiece sent the e-mail, it wasn't from the computer store. Not that we have any reason to think Keith or his dad helped someone send it, other than the fact they'd know how to disguise its origin."

"Glen Phelps paid Mr. Spiece a visit this morning," Reese said. "Or at least attempted to."

"Are you serious? How do you know?"

"I saw him standing on the porch ringing the bell when I drove by on my way to Ted's."

Kaylee's heart raced. "He's apparently a good friend of Mr. Spiece's."

Reese's eyebrows lifted. "The kind of friend who'd want to dissuade you from harassing him about ancient history?"

"Maybe. Of course when you put it that way, I kind of feel like dirt for doing it. But what if that's not the only reason he doesn't want history revisited?"

"It's a lot of maybes," Reese said. "Did you find anything useful in the yearbook?"

"With everything that happened this morning, I haven't had

a chance to go through it yet. As it is, I'd better head back to the shop. Mary's only supposed to work a half day today." Kaylee climbed into her van.

Reese tapped on her window. After she rolled it down, he said, "Forgot to tell you what Mary found out about the guy in the pickup truck who was watching your shop."

Kaylee's pulse spiked. "Yes?"

"He claimed to be one of Ted Munk's bodyguards. Apparently Ted asked him to watch over you because of an earlier threatening note you received." The emphasis he put on *earlier* made it clear he wasn't happy to hear about either note secondhand.

"Oh. Right. He had mentioned something like that."

"I didn't realize you two were serious."

"We're not dating. He's a dozen years older than me and lives ten months of the year in D.C."

Reese shrugged. "He won't if he becomes governor and makes you his personal florist."

She laughed. "Mrs. Banks must've started spreading that rumor. I imagine she's proud to have the supposed future florist to the governor's mansion doing her daughter's wedding arrangements."

"Supposed, huh?"

"Trust me. I have no interest in leaving Orcas Island. I just moved here."

Reese was clearly unconvinced. His gaze drifted in the direction of Ted's estate. "Be careful. Congressman Munk is the kind of guy who always gets what he wants."

Kaylee smiled. "He doesn't want me. He only said that to help me secure the wedding contract."

"I'm just saying he might have other reasons he wants someone keeping an eye on you." And with that Reese strode across the street toward the Munk estate.

Great. Thanks for creeping me out even more.

She drove back toward the flower shop. Mulling over the fact that Keith's father had paid a visit to the Spiece house this morning, Kaylee detoured so she'd pass the computer store before reaching her shop.

At the sight of swirling emergency lights, she slammed on her brakes. Two cruisers barricaded the street.

Kaylee jumped out of the vehicle and pushed through the crowd, which was blocking her view of what was happening beyond the cruisers.

"Whoa, that's as far as you go," Deputy Brooks said, stopping her with an outstretched hand.

"What happened?" Kaylee spotted paramedics loading a victim into an ambulance parked behind a badly damaged car. "Who's hurt?"

"Phelps," Brooks said and moved away to stop another gawker from crossing the line.

Kaylee's chest churned with a slightly unpalatable mix of relief and gratefulness. She didn't want to wish ill health on anyone, but if Glen Phelps had been the one who'd sent her the creepy notes, it felt kind of like divine justice that he should suddenly fall ill.

DeeDee hurried up to Kaylee, her face flushed. "It was horrible. I thought his dad was going to have a heart attack."

"Whose dad?"

"Keith's. The poor man is in really bad shape. I think they're bringing another ambulance for him."

"Glen isn't who they just loaded into that ambulance?"

"No, that was Keith."

Kaylee's heart jolted. "Keith? What happened?"

"He sideswiped the lamppost and then almost hit someone in the crosswalk."

"Did he blow a tire?"

"No, he had some sort of seizure or something." DeeDee glanced sympathetically at the young deputy manning the scene's perimeter. "The deputies must be feeling pretty rattled. Just last night they had that DOA and now this."

Kaylee's breath stopped up in her chest. "They can't be connected," she whispered.

"No, of course not." DeeDee sounded surprised that it was even a possibility.

Kaylee pressed her hand to her chest, straining to pull in even breaths. Her chest physically hurt at the wild notion that gripped her.

DeeDee grabbed her arm. "Are you okay? You've gone white. Come to my shop and sit down."

The people on the sidewalk swam in Kaylee's vision as DeeDee led her to the bookstore. "Last night's DOA," Kaylee said shakily, "was Dwayne Matthews. I'd just talked to him a few hours before he died in that crash."

"I'm so sorry." DeeDee guided her to an armchair among the bookshelves and handed her a bottle of water. "I didn't realize you knew him."

"I didn't." Kaylee took a gulp of water. "I talked to him once, about Danny Lane. He knew stuff. And then this morning, I got an e-mail with a picture of his car smashed against a tree and a message saying that's what happens to people who don't heed warnings."

DeeDee's brow furrowed. "You mean don't drink and drive."

"That was the one Dwayne didn't heed, but I think they meant me—the warning about paying the price when you poke around where you shouldn't."

DeeDee sat back and expelled a breath. "Oh."

"Then a couple of hours ago, I visited Keith Phelps and questioned him about the e-mail. Asked him if he'd helped someone send it."

DeeDee's eyes widened. "You think this wasn't an accident?"

Kaylee hugged her middle, suddenly feeling nauseated all over again. "I think someone's trying to send me a message and they don't care who gets hurt."

"This is *not* your fault," DeeDee said firmly.

"Do you think I'm reading more into this than there is?" Kaylee asked hopefully. "Like when people read their horoscopes, then interpret everything that happens to them to fit the prediction?"

DeeDee's teeth dug into her bottom lip. "Coincidences do happen," she said, not sounding like she was certain this was one.

Images of other people she'd talked to paraded through Kaylee's mind. Ted. The Petal Pushers. Reese. What if this creep went after one of them next?

Except none of them knew who killed Danny.

Did Keith?

"Do they think Keith will make it?" Kaylee asked.

DeeDee nodded. "Oh yeah. I think he was already coming around when they loaded him into the ambulance."

Kaylee bolted to her feet. "I need to talk to him."

"I'm sure it'll be some time before you can do that."

"He's not going to make it, is he? You just said he was coming around because—"

"No, Kaylee. I wasn't just trying to make you feel better." DeeDee urged her to sit back down. "I meant the sheriff might have questions for him before he can see visitors. I'll ask one of the deputies to come in and talk to you, okay? You can tell them about your conversation with Keith, just in case there is some connection."

Kaylee nodded, snatched up the water bottle, and downed the rest. Then she prayed for Keith's recovery—and that it wasn't her fault he might be fighting for his life.

13

Kaylee sat in one of the armchairs in Between the Lines, glancing from the front window to the covers of the books on display. Titles included *Delivered Unto Death* and *Deceived to Doom*. "These book titles are not helping," she said as DeeDee returned.

"Eddie is on his way." DeeDee turned down *Delivered Unto Death* and propped up *Mr. Cane Solves a Case*.

A shadow darkened the door, and Kaylee inhaled a fortifying breath.

Sheriff Maddox stepped into the shop and scanned the room.

Kaylee lifted her hand. "Over here."

"Is there a private room where I can interview her?" the sheriff asked DeeDee.

"Yes, my office. This way."

They followed DeeDee to a small room at the back of the store. "Take as long as you need," DeeDee said, then shut the door as she left.

Maddox pulled up a rolling office chair to face the one Kaylee had sunk into. "DeeDee tells me you think there's a connection between Keith's accident and Dwayne's."

"You saw the e-mail I got. It made it sound as if Dwayne's accident wasn't an accident."

Something about the muscle twitch in the sheriff's jaw heightened Kaylee's fears.

"You've found something," she whispered.

He sighed. "Yes. An inspection of the car indicated the brake lines were dry. The lines were nicked. They could have been damaged in the crash and drained by the time the car was put on the hoist this morning."

Kaylee struggled to breathe. "Or they could've been cut." *Because Dwayne made the mistake of talking to me.* "Was there any sign of brake fluid at the scene or where the car was parked overnight?"

"No. But the lines were rusty. Hitting a rock or pothole could have caused them to go. The break in the line wasn't a smooth cut, and the metal was shiny in spots, suggesting it had been pinged by rocks."

Or maybe not by a rock. Kaylee took a deep breath. "I spoke to Keith Phelps a few hours ago. Now he's in the hospital. That's an uncomfortable coincidence, don't you think?"

"Keith lost control of his vehicle because he panicked over a couple of bees in his car," Sheriff Maddox said. "He says he started to pull over so he could let them out, because he's allergic. The next thing he remembers is coming to as he was about to plow down a pedestrian."

"What made him lose consciousness before that?"

"He hit a pole and the air bag discharged, likely causing him to lose a few seconds' memory. He has no recollection of hitting the pole, or of anything between starting to steer toward the curb and waking up to a pedestrian screaming in front of him."

"So how did he hit the pole?"

"We don't know for sure. I suspect in his panic over the bees he hit the gas instead of the brake and oversteered toward the curb. He was stung. His father recognized the symptoms and administered his son's emergency dose of epinephrine."

"So whoever did this to Keith must have known he was allergic to bees."

The sheriff sighed. "No one did this to him, Kaylee. Bees get into cars all the time. Besides, think about it. If your e-mail writer was truly worried about Keith exposing him, he would have chosen a surefire way to silence him, not broken into his car and planted a couple bees on the remote chance it might do him in."

"Good point," Kaylee had to admit.

"Although you should heed the guy's warning," he added, "and leave the investigating to the professionals."

"But you're *not* investigating Danny's death."

"Which is another reason I suspect your e-mail writer is merely playing with you. If he's worried your snooping will expose him, why not simply kill you?"

Kaylee shuddered. "Maybe because I don't have a drinking problem or a bee allergy to conveniently blame for my untimely death."

"But he had to know you'd contact us. Why risk making us think we'd missed something in our investigations?"

"Maybe he didn't think that far ahead."

"He thought enough to use newsprint so you wouldn't have his handwriting and to cover his electronic tracks with the e-mail."

"I don't know what to tell you." Kaylee spun out of her chair and paced the small room.

"How about you start with who you think killed Danny?"

Kaylee stopped in front of the window and wrapped her arms around her middle. It was one thing to debate suspect possibilities amongst her fellow Petal Pushers, but to blurt them out to law enforcement without any proof felt wrong. "I have no proof."

"Tell me anyway."

She explained about the Brewer spruce on Mr. Spiece's former property.

The sheriff shifted. "So you think Mr. Spiece killed Danny?"

"He and Neil had the strongest motives if they thought Danny killed Joelle. But they both left the island early this morning. I guess they could've sent the e-mail from off-island and put the bees in Keith's car before they left, but how could they know I'd talk to him?"

"What did you talk to Keith about?"

Kaylee explained her theory about the e-mail. "Keith was hiding something. I'm sure of it. I thought it was who he helped to send the e-mail." She shook her head. "Then I wondered if Keith's dad sent it. He's a good friend of Joelle's dad. Reese told me he saw Glen knocking on Mr. Spiece's door this morning."

"You think Glen Phelps could have killed Danny?" From Maddox's tone, he clearly couldn't see it.

"He wasn't a frail old man three and a half decades ago. And he already blamed Danny for vandalism." Kaylee gestured helplessly. "But he wouldn't have put bees in his son's car."

The sheriff snapped his notepad shut. "I appreciate you advising us of your concerns. You can rest assured we'll investigate both incidents thoroughly."

Kaylee slumped back into DeeDee's office chair as Sheriff Maddox left. Had she been suspecting the wrong people? Reading too much into their reactions to her? *I can't see Mr. Spiece condoning endangering his friend's son either.* Maybe Keith's accident really was an accident.

DeeDee poked her head inside the office. "You okay?"

"Yeah. I'd better get back to the shop. Mary will be worrying about what's keeping me."

"I already updated her. She called to ask what was going on when she saw all the emergency lights."

Kaylee said goodbye to DeeDee, then left the bookstore. The street was still cordoned off between where she had parked the delivery van and The Flower Patch, so she had to take another street around.

On the second turn, she got to thinking about Dwayne's drained brakes and the weather forecast for rain this evening.

She pulled over and texted Mary, who quickly agreed to stay later than originally planned. Kaylee pulled back out onto the road and detoured to the country club to see if she could spot a stain of brake fluid in their parking lot before the rain washed it away. She had noticed some of the members actually had designated parking spots. If she was lucky, Dwayne had been one of the guys who'd wanted all the perks. She turned into the lot and scanned the names in empty spots along the two rows of designated spaces.

"There it is." She parked and did a search on her smartphone for the color of brake fluid, but was disheartened to discover that it was almost clear or yellowish when new, getting darker as it aged. It would be nearly impossible to see against the pavement. She read up on other common fluid leaks and decided if she found a puddle soaked into the ground, she might be able to figure out what it was by a process of elimination.

She pocketed her phone and went over to investigate. She found not one, but two stains. If both brake lines had suddenly started leaking, that sure didn't sound like an accident. The ground didn't appear green like antifreeze, or smell of gas. She touched the still damp spots and they felt slightly oily. Sheriff Maddox needed to know, but somehow she didn't think he'd be happy to hear she'd immediately gone off and followed up on his brake fluid revelation. She snapped a picture of the parking space with her phone, being sure Dwayne's nameplate was visible.

"Oh there you are!" Mrs. Banks appeared, flapping her arm out of her BMW at Kaylee. "When I saw your shop's delivery van, I hoped I'd find you. I had another idea for Chelsea's reception. Hold on a second."

Kaylee swallowed a groan.

Mrs. Banks pulled into a space two spots down the row and then hurried toward Kaylee. "Come on into the clubhouse and I'll show you." She shoved a navy blazer into Kaylee's hand. "But you'll need to put this on."

"Pardon me?"

"We have a dress code and that T-shirt won't pass."

Kaylee was wearing one of the brightly colored T-shirts she'd commissioned to advertise the store, but as she looked around, she realized even the golfers wore collared polos at the very least. She had dressed up for her presentation in the country club's dining room the other day, but she realized that she should make sure she wore appropriate clothing for any future visit she made, no matter where she'd be at the club.

"You know if you dressed professionally whenever you're out and about, you would attract a more affluent clientele. I have to admit that I'm a little concerned Congressman Munk's sweet spot for your shop has more to do with his fond memories of working there as a youth than the quality of your work."

Ouch.

Mrs. Banks fluttered her fingers at a couple of women practicing on the putting green. "This is the florist I was telling you about."

Kaylee pasted on a smile as one stage-whispered to the other, "She's the one the congressman was playing golf with, isn't she?"

Kaylee quickened her step, beginning to wish she'd never met Congressman Munk.

Twenty minutes later, her mind whirred with all of Mrs. Banks's new ideas. On her way out of the clubhouse, Kaylee glanced once more at the photographs of former club champions lining the hallway. When she reached the one of Ted's father, she stopped and did a double take. "That's Danny," she said aloud. She pressed her fingers to her lips and glanced around, but no one seemed to have heard her.

Why didn't Ted tell me Danny was his father's caddy?

Then again, she supposed Ted might have been embarrassed by the fact. Or maybe he just assumed she'd recognize him. But she hadn't seen a picture of Danny until Reese brought over the school yearbook this morning.

As she walked out to her van, a club employee was removing Dwayne's nameplate from his parking space. *Boy, they didn't waste any time.* She pulled up the photo she'd taken on her phone and quickly typed a carefully worded e-mail to the sheriff about happening to notice what could be brake fluid residue while visiting the country club to meet with a client. She added a warning that they were already changing the name on the space, so he might want to hurry.

Feeling guilty that she'd left Mary with the brunt of the work for yet another day, Kaylee rushed back to The Flower Patch. Bear must've recognized the sound of the van, because she could hear his happy welcome-home bark through the window as she climbed out.

Ted sauntered over from Death by Chocolate before she made it inside. "Hey, I caught a beautiful silver salmon out on the water today. Just got back twenty minutes ago. Would you like to help me eat it tonight?"

Kaylee's face grew hot. Fresh-caught salmon sounded delicious, but would he ask her to dinner if his interest weren't romantic? Reese's warning that the congressman always got what he wanted flashed through her mind. She sure didn't want to give him any misguided encouragement. "I'm afraid I've been out so much lately that I'm way behind on flower orders. I need to get my next one figured out tonight."

A hint of irritation crossed Ted's face, but he quickly masked it. "Of course. Business comes first."

She had the uneasy feeling that if she annoyed him too much, he might withdraw his favorable endorsement and Mrs. Banks would no doubt be thrilled to drop Kaylee like a hot potato, even if it meant forfeiting her deposit. Which reminded her, she needed to record Mrs. Banks's latest requests before she forgot them.

"I'll see you around." Ted pressed the key fob in his hand and the doors on the black SUV at the curb unlocked with a click.

"Not driving your convertible today?" Kaylee asked.

"No, it had to go into the shop." He opened the driver's side door then turned back toward her. "I almost forgot. My bodyguard mentioned that you didn't want him watching out for you."

Heat returned to Kaylee's cheeks. "I didn't realize that's what he was doing, or that he was working for you. Mary and I noticed him sitting in front of the shop for a long time and got a little unnerved."

"Right. My fault. I should've told you. I can send him back."

"Thank you, but no." For half a second, she debated telling him about the e-mail. Maybe he'd change his mind about putting political pressure on the sheriff to reopen Danny's case. But then he'd insist she use his bodyguard.

And she was no longer sure that she didn't need one.

14

The next morning, Kaylee walked into Death by Chocolate and Jessica greeted her with a new treat to try—a chocolate-peanut butter cupcake.

"Mary and DeeDee filled me in on what happened yesterday," Jessica said, handing Kaylee a bite-size sample of her new creation. "How are you feeling?"

Kaylee glanced around the coffee shop to make sure no one was listening in, then leaned closer to Jessica. "I feel as if I'm endangering anyone I talk to."

"None of what's happened is your fault. You're just trying to find the truth."

"Yeah, and now I can't even talk to Keith to find out if he thinks those bees were planted in his car."

"Why not?"

"I'm afraid whoever's watching me will go after him again." Kaylee ate the small bite of cupcake and hummed appreciatively. "This is amazing, Jess."

"I thought so too," Jessica said with a wink. "Anyway, I can talk to Keith for you. I have lots of help in the shop today, so I have the time. I'll take him a get-well package. Nothing like a little chocolate to get someone to spill his guts."

"That would be awesome. Take him one of these cupcakes and he'll sing like a canary." Kaylee coached her on what to say.

"I'll go right now," Jessica said. "DeeDee said she heard he'll be released before the end of the day."

"Wait." Kaylee grabbed her arm, entertaining another thought.

"Do you think he'd be reckless enough to stage the accident to take suspicion off himself?"

"No way." Jessica pried Kaylee's hand from her arm and handed her a mug with a bag of tea in it. "Add some hot water to this. I think you need it. The man was in anaphylactic shock. He could've died."

"That's what his father told the paramedics, but maybe they staged that too."

Jessica shook her head. "Don't overthink it."

Kaylee sighed. Sure, it sounded crazy, but it was way more palatable than thinking some nut planted bees in his car. Never mind stressing over what that nut might do next.

Then again, if he didn't do something to show his hand, she wouldn't be able to prove he had something to do with Danny's death.

Disheartened, Kaylee bid farewell to Jessica. Outside the bakery, she coaxed Bear away from the clutch of children showering him with attention and then headed into the flower shop. "I want to get lots done today," she said to Bear. She set her mug on the counter and cocked her head at the odd trickling sound coming from nearby.

Bear whined as she walked around to investigate the source.

"You hear it too, boy? It sounds as if it's coming from the basement." She opened the basement door and flipped on the light. "Ugh!"

Two inches of water covered the basement floor, and it was still rising.

She started down the stairs. To think she'd spent half the night worrying about someone doing something to her cottage. "How did he get in here?"

Bear sat at the top of the stairs and whined.

"Kaylee?" Reese called from somewhere in the shop. Then

his shadow darkened the steps. "Kaylee, stop! Don't step in the water."

Stepping past Bear, he reached over her shoulder and slapped off a switch in the basement ceiling.

"What does that do?" Kaylee asked.

"Turns off the power to the furnace. If the water reaches the furnace's relay and it has power on it, you'll be electrocuted."

Suddenly feeling faint, Kaylee swayed a little on the steps. "Thank goodness you came in when you did."

Reese steadied her. He smelled of soap and coffee. "You would've been all right for a bit. The furnace's relay is almost a foot off the ground." He slipped past her and forged through the water.

Kaylee started after him. "To think I just told the sheriff yesterday that my crazy note writer would have a hard time making my death look like an accident. I guess he's proved me wrong." She felt a whole lot more angry than scared now.

Reese twisted off a tap and the sound of rushing water stopped. "This wasn't attempted murder. Your hot water tank blew a hole. Probably thanks to the improved pressure of the new well pump."

"Really?" She felt a little silly for assuming the worst. Not that the situation wasn't terrible enough. "So now I have something else to repair on top of bailing the basement?"

"I can do that for you."

She shook her head. "That's okay. I'm sure you have lots of work waiting for you. I'll call George back in to take care of this."

"At least let me bring in my utility vacuum and give you a hand getting the water out." He was halfway up the stairs before he finished the sentence.

"Thank you," she called after him. She pulled out her cell phone and called her plumber, who said he could stop by around noon to assess the situation.

Bear padded down the stairs to investigate and seemed to decide he liked the new indoor water park. He frolicked and splashed in the water, soaking Kaylee to the knee.

"At least someone's happy," Kaylee said to Reese when he returned with his vacuum.

Reese looked at Bear and chuckled, then said, "It won't take long to get this up." He flipped on the machine and set to work. After a couple of minutes, he flipped the switch to off and removed the top. "I'll have to empty it frequently or it'll be too heavy to dump." He carried it to the old cement sink which had a pump beneath it to send the water up a pipe and out of the basement.

"It'd be a whole lot easier if this place had a sump pump hole." Kaylee scanned the basement floor. "It doesn't even have a floor drain."

"At least it's not the original dirt floor, or you'd be walking in muck."

"There's my silver lining." Kaylee hefted a couple of cardboard boxes onto a workbench to get them out of the water. She liked that Reese was a glass-half-full kind of guy, not to mention that he was willing to jump right in and do whatever needed doing whenever anyone was in trouble.

He continued vacuuming and dumping, and she kept clearing the floor of soggy boxes.

"Hello?" a shrill, too-familiar voice called from upstairs. "Anyone here?"

Kaylee swiped her damp hands down her slacks and sprinted up the stairs. Bear raced past her, leaving a trail of wet paw prints through the store.

"Oh my." Mrs. Banks's look of distaste shifted from Kaylee's soggy dog to Kaylee's soggy slacks. "It really isn't professional to have a wet, smelly animal running about your shop." She pressed the tops of her fingers to her nose.

"I apologize. My hot water tank blew last night and we're getting it mopped up."

"Hmm."

"How can I help you?"

Mrs. Banks waved off the question. "Never mind. I can come back when you're not so . . . busy." She gazed down her nose at Bear one last time, then click-clacked out of the store on her expensive heels.

Returning to the basement, Kaylee said, "If not for the congressman's endorsement, I'm sure that woman would have blackened the shop's reputation across the island by now for all the ways I dare to behave."

Reese shot her a bewildered expression. "What are you talking about?"

"You know, things like having a body in my backyard, or—gasp—wearing a T-shirt to the country club, or having a flood in the shop's basement. Totally unprofessional, don't you think?"

Reese laughed. "I've had a few clients like that. But I guess we all have our idiosyncrasies."

"Yeah, I'm really not complaining. Even my most demanding clients don't compare to the stress I had in my last job. It just helps to vent sometimes."

"Feel free. I don't mind." He dumped another load of water down the sink. "That takes care of the bulk of it. I need to get going, but I can leave the vacuum with you to finish up. I'll stop by for it later."

Kaylee walked him out, thanking him profusely for his help, especially when she realized he'd been at it for almost an hour. She was a little wary of using the vacuum with no one else on duty in the store for fear of not hearing a customer come in. She turned to Bear, who'd curled up on his bed, apparently deciding he'd had enough playtime for one morning. "Can I count on you to come get me downstairs the second someone comes through the door?"

He cocked his head.

Maybe it wasn't the most reliable plan. She knew she could count on him to bark, but she wasn't sure she'd hear it over the vacuum. "Maybe I'll mop up what's left. It's quieter." She rummaged around in the utility closet for her bucket and mop. Returning to the front of the store, she sniffed the air. "You really do make the place smell like wet dog." She took half a dozen of her most fragrant roses out of the storage cooler and set them in a vase on the counter. "Hopefully that will help."

Mopping was much slower than vacuuming, but Kaylee managed to sop up two dozen buckets of water before her canine alarm system notified her of a customer's arrival. She dropped her mop and raced up the stairs. "Oh, Jess, it's you." Kaylee glanced at the clock, surprised a couple of hours had already passed since Jessica had left for the hospital.

"What's going on?" Jessica asked, doing a dance with Bear to avoid him jumping up on her ivory pants.

"Bear, stay down," Kaylee ordered.

He pouted at her and slunk back to his dog bed.

"He only ever tries to jump up on you. I don't know what it is."

"It's because I smell like yummy baked goods." Jessica stooped down and ruffled Bear's floppy ears. "Don't I? Sorry I didn't bring a treat for you today." She stood and returned her attention to Kaylee. "Why's his bed all wet?"

"My hot water tank sprang a leak, and he was playing in the flood earlier."

"Oh wow. Let me give you a hand." She tucked her purse behind the counter. "And I can tell you about my visit with Keith."

"That'd be great." Kaylee grabbed a second mop.

"First of all, Keith leaves his car unlocked," Jessica said, following Kaylee to the basement. "So it is possible that someone snuck a couple of bees into his car, but he claims he couldn't fathom who would. He actually laughed when I floated the theory."

"He still denies someone used him and the store's VPN to send me an e-mail?"

"Yup. However, he did say that several of the computers on display have Internet access, and that someone browsing in the store could have logged into an e-mail account without him noticing. He called his dad and asked him to check each one's browsing history."

"I thought the point of a VPN was that it wouldn't keep track of where you've been."

"Yeah, I asked the same thing. He said they have a logger on their system, so they can see traffic, but the info is encrypted. What was interesting was that one of the computers' histories had been expunged."

Kaylee's mop jolted to a stop. "So someone could've sent an e-mail, then deleted their browsing history?"

"Exactly. And even though Keith had no idea who did it, your e-mailer may have been worried Keith would check into it after you talked to him."

"Did Keith figure it out?" Kaylee emptied the water from her bucket and resumed mopping.

"Not that he said."

"But you think he knows?"

Jessica shrugged. "I asked if the store had surveillance footage that might help. He called his dad again, and his dad said they must've had an electrical spike or something, because the system's memory had been corrupted."

"That sounds fishy. Keith let me see it yesterday. I didn't recognize anyone except what I thought was the back of Mr. Spiece."

"Didn't you say Keith's dad and Mr. Spiece were good friends?"

"Yeah, so it makes sense that he'd cover for him. Especially if Keith told him about my visit yesterday morning, or if he overheard something about it when the sheriff went to the hospital to question Keith."

Jessica shook her head. "I can't believe Glen would put bees in his son's car though. Or be on board with anyone else doing it."

"Neither can I. Maybe it was just a coincidence."

Bear let out a yip, and Kaylee welcomed the excuse for a break. Jessica joined her upstairs and browsed through the yearbook Reese had brought while Kaylee helped an elderly gentleman choose an arrangement for his wife for their sixtieth anniversary the next day. "Would you like it delivered?" Kaylee asked.

"No, I'll take it with me."

"Then I'll assemble it right away. It will take about fifteen minutes."

"Grand. I'll come back after I've been to the hardware store."

"Mr. Jacobs is such a sweet man," Jessica said after he left. "He comes into my shop every Friday afternoon and buys his wife a pastry. And he can't even eat them because he's diabetic."

Kaylee watched the elderly gentleman pass by outside the window.

"You know, if you accepted more dates, you might find Mr. Right yourself," Jessica said.

"What are you talking about? I had that golf date with Congressman Munk this week."

"I thought that wasn't a date. Besides, you declined dinner in favor of a night with the Petal Pushers."

"What can I say?" Kaylee grinned. "You guys know how to have a great time."

Jessica continued flipping through the yearbook as Kaylee assembled the anniversary arrangement.

"Hey, did you see this picture of Ted from his pre-politics days? He is a hunk." Jessica pointed to the page she was on.

Kaylee glanced at the picture of a teenage Ted holding up a gleaming trophy. "What did he win?"

"A boat race. You'll never guess who came in second."

"Who?"

"Keith Phelps. He was a freshman when Ted was a senior. I bet Ted would've hated to lose to him."

"From what I hear, he hates to lose period. I had to throw my golf game just so I wouldn't lose his endorsement to Mrs. Banks."

Jessica laughed. "Yeah, right. Mary told me you lost all but one of her golf balls."

"Oops, I forgot. I need to buy her replacements."

"Don't worry about it," Mary said, startling them both.

"Whoa, where did you come from?" Kaylee glanced from the front door to Bear, who hadn't barked.

"I snuck in the back."

Kaylee gave her a mock disapproving face. "This is supposed to be your day off."

"I brought some pots from home I want to do arrangements in. That okay?"

"Of course."

Mary peered over Jessica's shoulder at the yearbook. "That's one race Ted probably wouldn't have won if Neil had still been in it."

"Really?" Kaylee and Jessica said as one.

Mary nodded. "Sure. Everyone knew Neil had the fastest boat. But he sold it after Joelle's accident and never raced again."

Kaylee gaped at Jessica. "Are you thinking what I'm thinking?"

15

"I'm thinking Ted would've been very happy to see Neil's boat get damaged before the big race," Jessica informed Mary and Kaylee across the flower shop's workbench. "Maybe happy enough to pay a poor kid to ram it."

"Danny did say he was coming into a lot of money," Kaylee said.

"He did? How do you know that?"

"Dwayne told me the afternoon before he drove his car into a tree." She poked a couple more flowers into the arrangement she was working on as a wave of guilt resurfaced. Then an even more important connection occurred to her. "And Ted saw me talking to Dwayne. Not to mention, I found out yesterday that Danny was Ted's dad's caddy for the club championship that year, a fact Ted neglected to divulge. And he wasn't driving his car today. Said it had to go into the shop."

"Oh wow," Mary said. "Something tells me our congressman had another reason for putting his bodyguard on you."

Kaylee struggled to tamp down the anger welling up in her chest. "He might've asked me to join him for the golf game just so he could figure out what I knew and if I planned to keep on digging."

Jessica shook her head. "I don't know. It fits, but Ted isn't stupid." She tapped the picture of him in the yearbook she held. "I mean, sure, I can see the competitive teenager using Daddy's money to pay off a classmate to wreck his prime contender's boat. After all, money was what got him the QB spot on the football team, right? Maybe it was even his dad's idea. But the fact is, if they were behind Joelle's accident, they got away with it."

"Back then," Kaylee said. "But now he's worried about being exposed."

"Sure," Mary said. "But Congressman Munk isn't an impulsive teenager anymore. I doubt he would've risked doing anything that might bring more attention to a case the police were ready to close almost as soon as it was opened."

"Unless he had a nagging doubt that he left behind some critical piece of evidence," Jessica pointed out. "Like maybe DNA? Hearing Kaylee was a forensic botanist could have spooked him."

"And since he's running for governor, he couldn't risk any suspicions being cast in his direction," Kaylee added.

Mary didn't look convinced. "That's what he pays spin doctors for. I'm sure they deal with scandals meant to dethrone him on a weekly basis."

Jessica sighed. "She does make a good point."

Kaylee suddenly felt deflated. "I guess, but the theory is believable, don't you think?"

"It doesn't explain Danny's death," Mary said.

"Sure it does. Ted would've hired Danny to disable Neil's boat, not to kill anyone. Danny would've been feeling guilty over Joelle's death. He'd have wanted to talk to someone, and Ted would have wanted him to keep quiet."

Struck by the thought of what such a revelation would do to her grandmother, Kaylee accidentally crushed the flower she'd been inserting into the arrangement. She discarded the broken bloom for another and shut down the mental image of her grandmother at home in Arizona, fretting over what she might've done differently. "Think about it. Ted would've been afraid Danny would spill the whole scheme. Because, guaranteed, Danny wasn't willing to be the fall guy. So Ted could've been facing accessory to murder, accessory after the fact, withholding information, and who knows what else. Enough to put him away for a long time."

"Whereas bumping Danny off took care of all Ted's problems," Mary said.

"Exactly." Kaylee nodded. "Then Danny couldn't blackmail him for hush money. He couldn't expose him and, as a bonus, his disappearance confirmed his guilt in everyone's mind."

Jessica began to pace. "Say Ted was worried about DNA evidence. The simplest remedy would've been to take you out."

Kaylee shuddered. "I guess I should be thankful you didn't kill Danny."

"You know what I mean though."

"Yes, the sheriff said almost the same thing about my letter writer. He thinks it's someone playing with me. But I can't think of a single person I've offended . . . unless you count offending Mrs. Banks's sense of professional etiquette."

Mary chuckled, then immediately clapped a hand over her mouth. "I'm sorry. There's really nothing funny about any of this."

"No," Kaylee said with a sigh. "And as much as I hate to say it, my more urgent concern at the moment needs to be getting the last of the water mopped up and clearing out the soggy boxes before anything gets ruined." She glanced at the clock. "George could be here in less than an hour."

"What are you talking about?" Mary asked.

Kaylee filled her in on the shop's latest plumbing saga. "I know it's supposed to be your day off, but do you think you could keep an eye on the shop until I finish down there?"

"No problem. I was going to stay and create the new arrangements anyway."

"I can keep helping too," Jessica said.

By the time George arrived an hour later, the basement floor was damp but free of standing water, and all of the soggy cardboard boxes had been emptied and their contents piled onto shelves and benches for later sorting.

Jessica held up a long, rusty bar that had a hinged part on the end with a small, square post protruding from it. "What's this?"

Kaylee took the object to examine it more closely and was surprised by how heavy it was. "Nothing to do with gardening. The end piece looks as if it's for sockets, but there's no ratchet mechanism on it. For all I know, it could be for something totally different." She showed it to George. "Do you know what it is?"

George glanced up from examining the hot water tank. "It's a breaker bar. Like a lug wrench for changing tires, but you can put any size socket on it you want. Your grandfather probably had it for one of his old delivery vans." George tossed a wrench back into his toolbox and straightened. "As for this," he said, tapping the tank. "You're in luck. I have another one of this make in stock. I'm booked solid for the next few days, though. How desperate are you for hot water?"

Kaylee shrugged. "Actually, now that we've stopped the flood, getting a replacement isn't urgent. It's not as if the plants need hot water. We can wash our hands in cold water for as long as we need to."

He penciled her in for the following week and then headed off to his next client.

"Perfect," Jessica said. "This calls for a celebration. I'll grab us lunch from my shop." She passed Reese at the door as she rushed out.

"How goes the battle?" he asked good-naturedly.

"We're done," Kaylee said with a smile. "I'll get your vacuum."

He held up his hand, stopping her. "I can do that."

The shop phone chose that moment to ring, and she let him go ahead so she could answer it.

"Kaylee? This is Randy. I thought you might want to know that Digger is back in town."

"Oh." Surprised at the reason for his call, she hesitated for a few moments. "Thank you. I appreciate the heads up."

"The thing is," Randy added, sounding wary, "Bob told him you came around asking after him, and then Digger stormed out of here."

"That doesn't sound good." Kaylee looked at Mary, who had edged closer, her expression worried. "I appreciate you letting me know."

"No problem. You want me to say something to him?"

"Thanks, Randy, but it'll be fine." At the sound of the front door opening and Bear's accompanying yip, Kaylee jumped. She relaxed when she saw it was only the elderly customer returning for his anniversary bouquet. "A customer just walked in. I need to go. Thanks again for calling." She hung up, then smiled at Mr. Jacobs. "Your arrangement is all ready for you." She turned to collect it and almost slammed into Reese.

His gaze shifted from Mr. Jacobs to her. "Everything okay?" he asked, concern in his tone.

"Yes, just a pickup." Her voice sounded artificially high even to her own ears. She quickly gave Mr. Jacobs his arrangement and wished him a happy anniversary as he left.

Reese waited next to the counter until the door closed behind the older gentleman. "You all but jumped out of your skin when that guy walked in. What's going on?"

"You noticed that, huh?"

"Hard to miss."

"It was because of the phone call. Neil is back on the island and apparently wasn't happy to learn I'm still trying to get him to talk to me."

"And you're worried he's going to come for you?" Reese asked.

Kaylee chuckled. "I guess that sounds silly." She shook her head. "Especially when we'd just finished theorizing how Danny's killer might not be Neil or Mr. Spiece at all, but rather Ted." She told him about the picture Jessica found of Ted in the yearbook and explained their newest theory.

"I just thought of something," Jessica said, coming through the front door with lunch. "What if Neil killed Danny for revenge, like we first assumed, but then buried him in the flower shop's yard to frame Ted, since Ted was working here? Maybe Neil had an inkling Ted put Danny up to wrecking Neil's boat before the big race."

"You got all of that from a photo of Ted with a boating trophy?" Reese asked wryly, sounding as if he regretted bringing Kaylee the book to peruse.

Kaylee sighed. "We might've let our imaginations get away from us a little." Especially if Reese, who didn't even seem to like Ted all that much, thought the theory was far-fetched.

"I wouldn't go spreading rumors about Congressman Munk on nothing more than a hunch." Reese picked up his vacuum and turned toward the door. "Or the gentleman from Washington will slap you with a slander suit."

Kaylee cringed. "We won't."

"Maybe that's why the sheriff was so quick to close the case," Jessica said. "He must have known Ted worked here when Danny died. If that tidbit had come out in a news story, national reporters would've gone into a feeding frenzy." Her eyes lit up. "Maybe we could trick Ted into confessing."

"You're starting to sound like DeeDee." Mary helped Jessica set out paper plates on the counter and divvy up the sandwiches she had brought. "Bad guys only confess to you if they plan to kill you the next minute."

Kaylee's appetite faltered. "Maybe it's not a good idea for you two to hang around here."

"We're not leaving you alone when Neil Dykstra could walk through that door any minute," Jessica said.

They fell silent as they ate lunch, then puttered about the store, serving customers, working on orders, and sorting through wet stuff in the basement. After an hour passed with no sign of Neil, Jessica conceded she should get back to her own business.

By late afternoon, Neil was still a no-show, so Kaylee urged Mary to head home. "I have Bear here to protect me," she said.

Mary clearly didn't think he'd be much help. "Let me at least rig up that dash cam you bought before I go. It's not going to do you any good sitting in the box."

"I can help." Kaylee's Ford Escape was parked within view of the front door, so she'd be able to see if any customers came while they worked on it.

The ladies connected the camera, and Kaylee reviewed the basic operating procedures.

"I'm good to go with this," Kaylee said, hoping Mary was now confident she could be left alone. "Herb will be wondering what's keeping you."

Mary finally left a few minutes before closing time.

"I'm going to haul the wet boxes out back and then we can go too," Kaylee said to Bear.

Precariously balancing a stack of dripping cardboard, she nudged the back door open with her foot. Certain Jessica wouldn't mind her chucking them into the bakery's Dumpster, Kaylee hurried across to it.

Kaylee reached up to tip her burden over the bin's side.

A truck door slammed behind her. "What do you want from me?" an angry male voice demanded.

Kaylee's pulse jumped. *Was the guy talking to her?* She glanced over her shoulder, the boxes still suspended over her head. *Neil.* Her cargo teetered the wrong way. She squealed as water drops plopped in her hair.

Neil sandwiched her between himself and the Dumpster.

She screamed.

"Take it easy." Neil caught hold of the boxes.

She quickly ducked out from between his wall of muscle and the cold steel Dumpster as he hefted the boxes into the bin for her. "Sorry, I didn't realize what you were doing," she said. A safe distance between them restored, she planted her feet and faced him. "In answer to your ques—"

Frantic barks sounded from inside the flower shop.

Kaylee turned toward it. "Excuse me a sec. My dog is the only one manning my shop." Visions of Bear going ballistic on Mrs. Banks catapulted through Kaylee's mind. Even a congressman's endorsement couldn't undo that kind of damage.

Neil grabbed her wrist. "Not so fast."

16

"Let go of me." Kaylee yanked her arm free of Neil's grasp just as Bear raced from the store toward her. Or, more precisely, toward Neil. "Bear, no!" Kaylee ordered as the dog lunged for his ankle.

Bear stopped an eyetooth short of chowing down on Neil's work boot and growled instead.

Kaylee scooped him up. "It's okay, boy." To Neil, she added, "He must've heard my scream. He's surprisingly protective. What he lacks in size, he makes up for in spirit."

Neil didn't smile.

She was babbling she knew, but the man made her nervous. "What was with the arm grab?" she asked.

"You were the one who wanted to talk to me, then you look as if you're going to run off. What is your problem?"

She shifted from one foot to the other, only now realizing how over the top her reactions must've appeared to him. "I didn't realize Bear was barking for me. I was afraid he'd scare a customer. Why don't I just go around and lock up the shop, and we can talk over a coffee at the bakery?" Where Jessica and her customers could ensure all they did was talk.

"Something tells me I don't want to answer your questions in such close quarters with a bunch of busybodies."

Her heart hiccuped. "Fair enough." But she sure didn't want to talk to him in some secluded back alley. "How about we walk to the harbor?"

At his nod, she led him back to her shop, snapped a leash onto Bear's collar, and quickly locked up. For once, the salty breezes off the water and the mournful cries of gulls did nothing to calm her jittery insides. How was she supposed to broach the subject? *It seems to me that you and Joelle's father had the strongest motive to kill Danny. So, did you murder him?*

Neil saved her from the dilemma. "I don't think you appreciate how much your questions distressed Walter Spiece."

"Oh, trust me, I noticed."

Neil snorted. "And let me guess. You read it as guilt."

Kaylee shrugged.

"Well, let me set the record straight. Walter did not kill Danny."

"You know this for a fact?"

"Yes."

"How?"

"Because he told me."

"People lie all the time. Besides, if Walter didn't kill Danny, why did he get so agitated by my questions?"

Neil rolled his eyes as if she had the intelligence level of a toad. "Because if Danny didn't run away, then maybe he didn't kill Joelle either. Which means her killer could still be walking around out there." His intonation sounded more like a question, as though he couldn't understand what she didn't get about his theory.

Kaylee slanted a narrow-eyed glance at him. "How is that any different than thinking Danny got away with her murder and was walking around out there?"

"When the FBI couldn't find Danny, Walter assumed Danny was dead. Divine justice."

They reached the water and Kaylee faced Neil. "Again, how is that any different than finding out Danny was buried in the flower shop's yard?"

Neil gritted his teeth, the muscles in his cheeks rippling. He crossed his arms and stared at her for a long moment. He released an anguished sigh. "The truth is you had him worried I'd be charged."

Kaylee's heart thumped. "With killing Danny?"

"Yes."

"Did you?"

"No!"

Kaylee tilted her head and mirrored his crossed arms. "And I should believe you why?"

"Because all these years, I secretly wondered if Walter killed him."

"You thought he was a murderer, yet you remained good friends? Tended his lawn? Drove him to his daughter's home off-island?"

"He's Joelle's father." Neil's voice cracked. His gaze drifted to the distant horizon. "And she was the only woman I've ever loved."

"That justifies murder?"

Neil swiped the back of his hand at the corner of his eye, then shook his head. "No. But he's family. You take care of family, no matter what."

Kaylee conceded that much with a nod.

"Anyway, Walter didn't kill Danny. We talked a long time while I was driving him yesterday. That's when he confessed to being sure I killed Danny and being grateful for it, but scared for me. I assured him I didn't kill him, and admitted to having wondered if he had."

"But you had a scuffle with Danny in Walter's yard," Kaylee said matter-of-factly.

"No," he said, drawing out the word to convey how ridiculous the accusation was. "I barely knew the guy."

"You went to the same school."

"He was a year behind me. How many girls a year behind you in school do you remember?"

She thought about that a moment. "The ones that were in the same clubs as me."

"Well, Danny wasn't on the football team."

"Did Joelle's father mention getting into a fight with Danny?"

"No. Why would he? The sheriff never told us Danny was even a suspect until after the kid disappeared."

Kaylee cocked her head. "So you're saying Danny wasn't even on your radar? Then why would either of you have thought the other killed him?"

Neil raked his hand through his hair. "Everyone was speculating about suspects."

"Everyone? Including Walter's friend Glen Phelps?"

"Oh yeah. He thought it was Danny because the kid toilet-papered the tree outside his shop after he got kicked out of the store."

That was the vandalism Glen had been referring to? Kaylee had imagined something much worse. "Why did Danny get kicked out of his store?"

Neil shrugged. "He was probably playing a video game on one of the computers. No one had their own computers back then. Not that Danny would've anyway. His dad was a deadbeat."

"Was Glen Phelps at Walter's a lot?"

"I guess."

"So Glen could have had a run-in with Danny there?"

"Why on earth do you think Danny would come within a mile of Walter's place?"

Kaylee debated how much to tell him. "A piece of evidence found with Danny's remains places him at Walter's old homestead sometime before his death."

Neil's fingers fisted. "What evidence?"

Would he warn Glen if she told him? Then again, if he did, Glen's reaction would be telling. "Danny's clothes had a *Picea breweriana* cone caught in them, most likely from a scuffle on the ground."

"A *Picea* what? You're saying he had a pinecone on him?"

"Yes."

"So what? He could've just found the cone and stuffed it in his pocket. My sister was always collecting pinecones." Neil paused as if maybe his thoughts had shot in the same direction as Kaylee's—the cone could've fallen from the killer's pocket—and he'd just admitted to a close family member collecting them. Neil shoved his hands into his jacket pockets. "Lots of people collect pinecones."

"They do, but the *Picea breweriana,* or Brewer's spruce as it's commonly called, isn't native to this area. The old Spiece property boasts the only known one on the island."

"The only one now maybe," Neil said. If he'd had a moment's thought that Walter had fed him a story to conceal his own guilt, Neil didn't show it. "There could've been others thirty years ago. Whenever a new house goes up, trees come down."

"Let's forget about the cone for now. You must have some suspicion as to who killed Danny."

"I don't know. Joelle's death had the whole town worked up. The whole island really."

"Did you discuss possibilities with Walter?"

Neil's gaze drifted to the horizon. "After we got over our relief that neither of us were going to get shipped off to jail, we started to wonder if Danny's death might really have been divine justice. You know, he snuck around the shop, intending to break in, and tripped into the hole and smashed his head, like the sheriff said." Neil shrugged. "But like I said, Joelle's death had the whole town worked up. And it was easy to believe bad things about Danny. He was always getting into trouble."

"Do you remember who else was investigated at the time of Joelle's death?"

"Just about everyone with a boat. Especially the guys my age who liked to race. But their boats were all fine. At least none looked as if they'd rammed into mine"—he winced—"which was what Joelle was driving."

"You ever race Keith?"

"Sure. He had a fast boat."

"But Danny didn't have a boat."

"They figured he stole one from a summer islander who wasn't around to report it missing."

"Did anyone report a boat missing when they arrived come summer?"

Neil's gaze drifted over the boats moored in the harbor. "Not that we were told. I'd never thought of that before."

"Do you think it's possible the boat involved in the hit-and-run didn't sustain any damage?"

Neil frowned as if he were contemplating the possibility. "I guess it's possible. But there would've at least been paint marks on it. My boat was cherry red, and a ton of paint was scraped off of it."

Kicking her foot at the sand, Kaylee cleared a swath. The paint could've been buffed away before the sheriff's inspection almost as easily. The probability of solving this case with enough proof to make it stick was looking slimmer by the minute.

Neil exchanged glances with a guy leaning against a rail on the pier.

"Hey, isn't that Bob who works for you?" Kaylee asked.

"Yeah." Neil gave the guy a subdued midair wave and Bob shuffled off.

What was that about?

"So have I answered all your questions?" Neil asked.

"Let me be sure I have this straight. The only concrete evidence tying Danny to Joelle's accident is that someone saw him near the harbor that evening—on land?"

"I guess."

"Does that sound convincing to you?"

He didn't answer.

Kaylee let out a frustrated breath. "Don't you want to know who really caused Joelle's drowning?"

"We don't know it wasn't Danny." Neil picked up a stone and flicked it across the surf, causing it to bounce on the water several times before sinking out of sight. "I'm not sure her dad could handle it all being dredged up again. And I learned a long time ago that I needed to forgive and let go. It was an accident. Yeah, the culprit was a coward not to come clean, but if he's still alive, he's probably tortured himself more than the law could."

Kaylee thought Neil might be the most mature guy she knew. There was just one problem.

"Joelle's death might have been an accident, but I'm not ready to write off Danny's death as one."

17

Later that evening, Kaylee's cell phone ringtone pierced the air at Wildflower Cottage. At the sight of Bea's name on her phone screen, Kaylee hesitated to answer the call. She had more questions than answers—nothing that would ease her grandmother's anxiety. Yet ignoring the call certainly wouldn't ease Bea's mind either. Kaylee picked up and meandered to the cottage window overlooking the meadow and the ocean beyond—one of her favorite views.

"Hi, sweetie," Bea said. "I was about to give up on you answering. Any news?"

"What can you tell me about Glen Phelps?"

"Oh." The anxiety her grandmother imbued into that single word escalated Kaylee's suspicions of the man.

"What is it?" Kaylee prompted when her grandmother didn't elaborate.

"He could be the nicest man. A loyal friend. A very good husband. He was right at his wife's side through her battle with cancer."

"But?"

Her grandmother released a heavy sigh. "He is also the type to hold a grudge."

"And he had one against Danny?"

"Against Danny's father actually. He was a used-car salesman and he sold Glen a lemon. It conked out on the poor man when he was taking his wife to a specialist on the mainland."

"Is that why he pegged Danny as a troublemaker around town?"

Bea was silent for a long time. "Danny was a scrapper. Having a mother who skipped town and a father who sold used cars, he needed to be, I suppose. He was a good boy at heart. I don't think he was behind nearly as many incidents as Glen blamed on him."

"But the vandalism did stop after Danny disappeared?" That's what Glen had claimed.

"I wouldn't have called it vandalism," Bea said. "Just a bit of mischief. Seems to me they figured out later that the overturned garbage cans had been the work of a stray dog."

Yet Glen had seemed determined to make sure Kaylee knew Danny got what he supposedly deserved. "Did Glen ever visit the shop?"

"Oh yes. After his wife took ill, he bought a fresh bouquet for her every week."

"So he would've known about the hole in your side yard."

"You should check the archives of *The Orcas Gazette* at the library," Bea said, rather than answer Kaylee's question. "Back in those days, they used to chat about what people were up to around Turtle Cove—who was visiting from the mainland, who'd had a party, who was sick, that sort of thing. It's so long ago. I can't remember if Glen's wife had passed by then or not." Another heavy sigh hissed over the line.

"Try not to dwell on it, Grandma. I know you feel bad for what happened to Danny, but you were good to him. You gave him work when it sounds like nobody else would. I'm sure he wouldn't want you to make yourself sick over what can't be undone."

Her grandmother let out a humorless chuckle. "Yes, that's what Lucille says."

Kaylee was grateful Bea's twin sister was so supportive. Wanting to end their conversation on a lighter note, Kaylee said, "I forgot to mention the last time we talked that one of your former student employees stopped by to say hello."

"Who?"

"Congressman Munk."

"Teddy?" She laughed. "He pops by for a visit every summer. Is Raylene Nelson still tagging along everywhere he goes?"

"She sure is."

"She's been his number one cheerleader as long as I've known them. He doesn't appreciate her nearly as much as he should. Of course her support is probably because she's been head over heels for him since high school, but he could still show a little more gratitude."

Kaylee was about to ask if Danny and Ted worked at the shop at the same time, but decided against bringing up Danny again, not when her grandmother's mood finally sounded a little cheerier. "Well, I should go," Kaylee said. "Bear is getting into trouble in the meadow."

Kaylee disconnected the call and slipped outside, then called for Bear.

Instead of coming to her, he barked insistently at whatever he'd found. She couldn't see anything more than the tip of his tail waving above the grass. Most likely he'd come upon some small animal that didn't have the good sense to take off.

Kaylee meandered to the edge of the yard and summoned him again.

His yip turned to a low growl that sent a chill down Kaylee's spine.

"Who's out there?" Kaylee said in her most authoritative voice. "I'm calling the police."

Bear scampered toward her, and a moment later a ginger cat shot up a tree not far from where he'd been.

"Were you tormenting that poor kitty?" Kaylee scolded him, her heart still beating in double time. "You need to come inside while I visit the library."

Twenty minutes later, at the sight of Mrs. Banks's BMW parked outside the library, Kaylee hesitated. The woman hadn't been impressed with her state this morning. Kaylee looked down at her scoop-neck tee and faded jeans—definitely not up to Mrs. Banks's exacting standards. Then again, she worked with plants. What did the woman expect?

The door burst open, and Kathy Fitz emerged with two fistfuls of dead leaves. She dumped them over the porch rail behind a shrub. She looked up and noticed Kaylee on the sidewalk. "You're just the person we need. Our plants are dying and we don't know why. Come and see."

Kathy led her to a staggered grouping of tropical plants in front of one of the large front windows. The plants included everything from pothos to cactus. "You appear to have a few different issues here," Kaylee said. "It's a good idea to isolate the diseased plants and sterilize your tools before moving from one to the next, especially if they're afflicted with a virus. I'm afraid viruses are usually incurable."

"Is it a virus?"

Kaylee picked up a *Platycerium bifurcatum* with leaves that were yellow and wilting, and then she dug into the drenched soil to examine the roots. "This elkhorn fern has root rot. It needs a pot with better drainage, and you need to be careful not to overwater it."

"Huh," Kathy said, frowning. "We had a Boston fern whose leaves went all gray, and one of our patrons said it had root rot because we probably hadn't been watering it enough."

Kaylee nodded. "*Nephrolepis exaltata* are highly susceptible to graying. And it is caused by drought and can lead to root rot. It's really important to maintain even soil moisture at all times with ferns."

Next, Kaylee pointed to the yellow, brown, and black spots

on a couple of dracaena. "This is leaf spot. It's pretty common with dracaena and dieffenbachia. With the summer sun, this window has probably been too hot and humid for them." She moved the plants back from the window and put more space between them. "It's also a good idea not to crowd the plants. They need good air circulation."

Kaylee pulled a bird's nest fern with mottled leaves from the grouping and handed it to Kathy. "I'm afraid this *Asplenium nidus* has bacteria blight. You'll have to dispose of it before it can infect the others."

"How do we prevent it?" Kathy asked.

"Avoid overhead watering and ensure you start with disease-free plants." Kaylee pointed out the translucent spots. "This is how it starts, but the spots will quickly enlarge and turn reddish-brown with a purple halo."

"Wow, you really know your stuff," came the familiar voice of Chelsea Banks. She held the hand of an adorable kindergartner carrying an armload of picture books.

Kaylee shrugged. "My degree is in botany. I taught plant taxonomy at the University of Washington for years."

"Cool. Mom will be impressed to hear that." Chelsea turned to a young teen girl doing homework with a boy at a nearby table. "Only five more minutes." Returning her attention to Kaylee, she lifted the clasped hand of the little girl beside her. "This is my flower girl, Bailey. Bailey, this is Miss Bleu. Miss Bleu is making our bouquets for the wedding."

"Oooh!" the girl squealed, her ponytails bobbing. "Can I have snowflakes in mine?"

Kaylee shot Chelsea a questioning glance.

"She's a huge fan of a certain children's movie involving an ice queen," Chelsea said.

"I'll see what I can do, Bailey," Kaylee said, thinking the

Stephanotis floribunda that Mrs. Banks and Chelsea had picked out would do the trick.

"Thanks," Chelsea mouthed, handing the girl's books to Kathy to check out. "Eva, come on," she said to the girl at the table. "Time to go. The dress fitting is in ten minutes."

The teen girl and the boy beside her glanced from Chelsea to Kaylee then huddled over their table, whispering feverishly.

Kaylee recognized Eva as the visitor who'd taken Matt's bike for a joyride at Sunday's youth outing. But the boy beside her wasn't Matt.

Chelsea rolled her eyes. "I told her doing a guy's homework is not the way to win his heart, but what does a bride-to-be know? I'm just her cousin after all."

Kaylee smiled. "Have fun."

Kathy handed Bailey her books and shook her head as Eva trotted to catch up with Chelsea and Bailey. "We have at least one girl every year who tries to win a guy by helping him with his schoolwork. They don't seem to get that intelligence isn't always the trait guys that age are most drawn to."

A white-haired woman meandered up to the counter with a novel. "It was the same way when I was a teacher back in the day. The high school jocks were the worst for taking advantage of the smart girls."

"I guess I was too smart to let them take advantage of me," Kaylee quipped. "Then again, I'm also still single."

"Yeah, I still can't believe you blew off the congressman's dinner invitation in favor of the Petal Pushers." Kathy sounded flabbergasted.

Kaylee shrugged. "I'd like to look at the newspaper archives. Where can I find those?"

"I'll show her," a male voice said from behind her.

Kaylee spun around to see Deputy Nick Durham grinning

at her. "Thanks," she said with a smile Kathy was bound to misinterpret. But Kaylee and Nick were just friends, in spite of his reputation as a notorious flirt. Besides, he was a talented investigator, and she might be able to coax some inside information out of him.

Nick led the way to the basement stairs. "Let me guess. You're interested in what the townsfolk were up to thirty-five years ago."

"What can I say? I can't resist a good mys—" Kaylee swallowed the admission at the sight of Ted's bodyguard striding through the front door.

He wore dark sunglasses, so she couldn't see his eyes, but she was certain they were trained on her.

She hurried after Nick.

The bodyguard didn't follow.

Maybe he just liked to read. Or maybe he was still keeping an eye on her, even though she thought Ted would have called him off by now. Except if he was tailing her, was it really for her protection? At least she was safe with Nick.

Nick led her to an old microfiche machine and motioned for her to take a seat. A copy of a thirty-five-year-old spring edition of the *Gazette* was on the screen.

"You were already checking these out?" Kaylee asked.

"Yup, just stepped out for a quick supper break."

Kaylee smiled, pleased to know that at least one person in the sheriff's office wasn't ready to write off Danny's death as an accident.

"Deputy Brooks told me about your flat tires, and Maddox mentioned the notes you received."

Kaylee couldn't stop the heat that crept to her cheeks. As Nick well knew, it wasn't the first time since moving to Orcas Island that her curiosity had earned her some less-than-amiable attention.

"The sheriff told you Dwayne's brake lines were dry?" Nick said.

"Yes."

"Turns out he also had a cracked rear bumper. Not something a head-on collision would cause."

Kaylee's chest tightened. "So you think he had help going off the road?"

"Could be. Maddox said both Digger and the congressman saw you talking to Dwayne?"

"Yes."

"Digger's truck sits too high to have caused the bumper damage. But the heavy chrome bumper on Munk's Mustang could've easily done it and ended up no worse for wear."

"He was driving a different car the next day. Said the Mustang had to go into the shop."

"Interesting." Nick glanced at the stairs and lowered his voice. "If you ask me, Congressman Munk seems to have a little too much influence over our good sheriff." Nick pulled up a chair. "Let's see if we can find anything in here that'll shed some light on what was really going on thirty-five years ago."

They skimmed notations about everything from strawberry socials to new babies. The only mention of Ted was in articles about the high school football games. The only mention of Glen Phelps was in his store ads that graced every paper. "It's interesting to see how ads have changed over the years."

"Yeah, look at this one for Nelson's Mechanics Shop." Nick pointed to the top of the screen. "'We give you a break on brake repairs and won't hose you on radiator replacements.'"

"Cute." Kaylee moved on to the next week's paper, then the next week's, and the next. She cringed at the ads for Lane's Used Cars. His slogan was "making perfect matches," and the car photos all had blonde models posing on the cars' hoods. Kaylee could just imagine the ribbing Danny would've gotten over those.

Glen Phelps's ads appealed to a customer's desire for the

best stereo or latest tech gadget. At that time, VCRs and home computers were just becoming the next big thing. "Danny could've tried blackmailing Phelps."

"What was that?" Nick said before Kaylee realized she'd stated her musing aloud.

"I was thinking about who had motive to kill Danny. And it seems to me there are two camps. There are those out for revenge because they believed he caused Joelle's death. Or there are those he could've blackmailed because he didn't kill Joelle, but knew who did."

"I hadn't thought of that," Nick admitted.

"My grandmother said Danny was afraid of boats. And the way I figure, Joelle's death was either an utterly random accident, or someone specifically targeted Neil's boat or Joelle. I haven't heard of anyone having a beef with Joelle, but I suspect both Ted and Keith, as Neil's chief competition in the upcoming boat race, might've been tempted to damage his boat."

Nick nodded.

"According to Glen's interview in the paper about the accident, he was in Seattle at the hospital with his wife that night. If Keith wasn't with him, he was unsupervised the whole night."

"He got an underage drinking warning that night," Nick said.

"Really? I'm surprised that didn't make it into the paper."

Nick shrugged. "Phelps spent a lot of money on ads every year. Money that helped fund the editor's paycheck. Actually, a bunch of kids got warnings that night. There was a big beach party celebrating a football game win, and someone got their hands on some booze."

"Which could make kids do really stupid things."

Nick pushed to his feet. "I think I'll pay Keith Phelps a little visit."

"Mind if I tag along?" Kaylee asked.

"I should tell you no way, but I think you have as much info as I do on this case. I'll say you're along as a consultant. Some kind of unique grass that only grows in Keith's yard or something."

Laughing, Kaylee quickly returned the library's microfiche to its folders and grabbed her purse. "Any idea where Congressman Munk would take his car to be serviced? Because I was thinking we could stop by his mechanic's place to find out what work he needed done."

Nick held open the passenger door of his cruiser for her. "My guess would be Nelson's, since his daughter works for him. It'd be closed by now."

Raylene Nelson. Of course. Kaylee should've realized the connection. And a mechanic's daughter would've easily been able to advise Ted or one of his men on how to drain Dwayne's brake lines.

He'd sent a text just before they left the golf course, Kaylee recalled. Ted could have alerted Raylene to the potential damage Dwayne could do to their campaign. Then again, Keith and his dad owned an electronics store—who knows what kind of spyware they could've planted on Kaylee? Maybe that's why Glen had paid her that visit the day after Danny's remains were unearthed. She'd heard there were ways of loading spyware on phones without physically touching it. And guaranteed if there was a way, a tech geek like Keith would know how to do it.

Kaylee sighed.

Nick glanced across the seat at her. "What's wrong?"

"I hate thinking the worst about people on nothing more than a hunch."

"Don't beat yourself up. Sometimes a good hunch is what cracks a case."

18

Ten minutes later, Keith welcomed Nick and Kaylee into his home. "More questions? You still think someone put a bee in my car so I wouldn't talk?"

"We're not sure what to think," Nick said.

Aside from a welt on Keith's arm where the air bag's casing had probably struck it, he didn't seem any the worse for wear from his accident.

"How are you feeling?" Kaylee asked as he led them past the front room, stacked full of old computers, stereo systems, and VCRs.

"Much better." Keith stepped into his rec room and motioned them to a pair of leather recliners.

A gigantic TV screen and the latest and greatest in stereo equipment dominated the room. And surprisingly, given the obvious obsession with electronics, five-foot high stacks of old newspapers lined the back wall.

Keith lounged in a recliner, while Kaylee, her heart racing, pretended to admire the surround-sound setup to get a closer look at the newspapers. There were copies of the *Seattle Times,* the *New York Times,* the *Washington Post,* and who knew what others further down in the stacks—more than enough to choose from to make the note she'd been sent. She glanced about, hoping to spot scissors, glue, or a trash bin with cut bits of paper, but no such luck.

"Did Danny Lane try to blackmail your father?" Nick asked, wasting no time getting to the point of their visit.

"Ha! For what? Dad's as honest as they come. Danny would have had nothing to blackmail him about."

"But what if Danny had something on you? Something that might've sullied the store's reputation?"

Keith shook his head. "You talking about the underage drinking warning I got my senior year of high school? Half the kids in my class got one that night. It was no secret. After Joelle's accident, the first place they came looking for suspects was our party."

"What if Danny threatened to make more of your drinking? To imply it could've been you recklessly piloting the boat that rammed Joelle's?"

Keith snapped his recliner back to an upright position. "That's garbage. Who told you that?"

"Just a theory I'm working," Nick said coolly.

"I didn't even have a boat there. I got a lift with a friend."

"Who?" Nick asked.

"Bob Mackey."

Kaylee scarcely muffled her intake of breath. Bob had been working with Neil at the clubhouse the afternoon she talked with Dwayne. He could've warned Keith. Or run Dwayne off the road himself. She'd assumed he acted cagey around her because he was wary of her suspicions of Neil, but maybe he was just wary of what she'd expose. "Was Bob on the water at the time of Joelle's accident?" she asked.

"No, the party was in full swing by then."

"Where were you Tuesday night?" Kaylee asked.

Nick shot her a glance, eyebrow raised, obviously guessing that she was referring to the night of Dwayne's death.

"Bob was on Neil's crew at the clubhouse that day," she continued.

Keith didn't betray any awareness of the significance of that fact. "I volunteer at the hospice center every Tuesday evening."

"How about your father?" Kaylee asked.

"He doesn't drive anymore. He usually stays in and watches TV," Keith said.

Recalling what Mr. Fitzpatrick had said about the prowler in The Flower Patch's backyard squealing away in a loud vehicle, Kaylee asked, "Did you have a vehicle in high school?"

Keith shook his head. "Nope, I put my money into my boat."

Kaylee crossed her arms. "What did your parents drive?"

"A Pontiac powered by hamsters."

That didn't sound to Kaylee like a car that would be squealing away from the scene. "What did your friend Bob drive?"

"A motorcycle."

Mr. Fitzpatrick surely would have recognized the difference in sound between a motorcycle and a car or truck.

Nick stood. "Thanks for your time." He ushered Kaylee outside. "I don't think he's hiding anything. He didn't seem at all fazed by the questions."

"I agree." Kaylee checked the time. "I'd better get home. It's been a long day and I've got a slew of arrangements to make tomorrow for an evening wedding. Could you please drop me back at the library so I can get my car?"

"Sure thing."

Ten minutes later, Nick parked behind her car in front of the library.

The street was deserted.

Nick hopped out of the cruiser. "Let me check your car over before you get in."

Kaylee's heart missed a beat. She folded her arms across her chest and hugged her middle. If her note writer had seen her drive off with Nick earlier, he certainly wouldn't be under any illusion she was finally heeding his warnings.

Nick flicked on a small flashlight and shimmied under the

car. "No sign of any cut lines." He wriggled back out. "Pop the hood for me."

Kaylee obliged, and Nick tested the soundness of the wires and pipes.

"Looks good," he said, closing the hood. He flicked his flashlight over the interior, then moved around to the back. He opened the rear door and checked inside, then closed it. Finally, he peered in the tailpipe. Apparently satisfied, he stood. "All clear as far as I can tell. Want me to follow you home?"

Part of her wanted to say yes, but she didn't want to be a scaredy-cat. "That's okay. Bear's at home. He'll let me know if there's been anyone around."

"Call me if anything seems suspicious."

"I will, thanks."

A mile from home, Kaylee's vehicle started to sputter. The gas gauge read half a tank. She nudged the accelerator down a fraction more. *C'mon, just get me home.* She turned into her driveway and the vehicle died.

Relief she'd made it home safe and sound tempered the nagging feeling someone had hoped she wouldn't. Nick had checked the vehicle over thoroughly and found nothing amiss, but maybe the gas gauge was broken.

She dialed Mary's number. "Hey, is Herb busy tomorrow?"

"Not with anything that can't be put off. What's up?"

"My car just died. Thankfully it waited until I got home." Kaylee opened the cottage and let Bear out as she explained. "I don't think it's been tampered with, but I'd prefer to have someone I trust look it over before I pay to have it towed to a garage."

She heard Mary relay the situation to her husband in the background. "He'll be there at eight. Do you want me to give you a ride to work?"

"I can ride my bike."

"Okay," Mary said, her tone solemn. "But seriously, Kaylee—be careful."

19

Kaylee and Bear's morning ride to work was uneventful, but she still welcomed the excuse to hide out in her workroom all Friday morning, creating bouquets and boutonnieres for the Gilchrist-Everett beach wedding that evening.

Mary poked her head in around eleven. "Your favorite client is here."

Kaylee glanced up, pondering whom she meant. Reese was the first to come to mind, although he probably didn't qualify as a client. More likely Mary was teasing Kaylee about Ted. But Kaylee wasn't about to fuel the idea by naming him. "Who's that?" she said instead.

"How long is she going to make me wait?" Mrs. Banks's irritated voice carried from the showroom.

Chelsea's wedding isn't for another six weeks and her mother has already changed her mind on arrangements at least that many times. Kaylee groaned quietly.

Mary's eyes sparkled with amusement. "I'm just happy she only wants to deal with the owner." She took the boutonniere Kaylee was working on. "I'll finish this."

Kaylee hurried out to see what Mrs. Banks wanted this time. She found her and Chelsea waiting near the front display window.

The woman scowled at Kaylee's apron and Kaylee reflexively brushed at it, sending stray bits of stems and leaves fluttering to the floor. In her stomach, butterflies did a similar swirling dive.

Mrs. Banks held up a dainty crystal bowl the size of a teacup. "I found these and thought they would make lovely wedding favors."

"I was thinking we could plant each with a miniature rose or violet or something," Chelsea said.

Kaylee studied the bowl. "It isn't a good pot for a plant. There's no drainage, and the dirt would be visible through the clear sides. But I have another idea." She reached out her hand. "May I?" Mrs. Banks handed her the bowl and Kaylee led her to the aisle displaying DeeDee's selection of handcrafted soaps. She arranged a variety of miniature shell-shaped ones in complementary colors in the base of the bowl and propped a heart-shaped one on top. "Something like this might be nice."

"Ooh, I love it," Chelsea said. "And we can do them up ourselves."

Mrs. Banks actually smiled. "Splendid. We'll take enough of those soaps to fill 200 bowls."

Kaylee pulled out her pen and order pad. "I don't have that many in stock, but I can order them today and they should be ready within a week. Will that be okay?"

"That's fine."

Since the woman had a bad habit of changing her mind, Kaylee took a larger deposit than she normally would. Not that Kaylee needed to fret over it. Mrs. Banks seemed to enjoy buying things.

Kaylee returned to the workroom with a spring in her step. "I think I might finally be on Mrs. Banks's good side."

"I knew you'd win her over eventually. This order is all done. When does it need to be delivered?"

"I'll drive them around to the Gilchrists' midafternoon."

Bear let out a woof, alerting them to the arrival of another customer. Kaylee hurried out to offer her assistance. "Mr. Hornblower, nice to see you again. Visiting your grandchildren?"

"You bet. Not sure why we ever moved off the island considering how often we come back to visit. I hear you ran into some nasty business here a bit ago."

"Yes, I guess the victim would've been one of your former

students." Mr. Hornblower had been the island's high school principal for forty years before he retired. "Do you remember Danny Lane?"

"Yes, a bright boy. I never could believe he was responsible for Joelle's accident, never mind that Raylene Nelson noticed him at the harbor that night."

"Raylene was the witness?"

"As I recall, yes."

Given Raylene's supposed crush on Ted, Kaylee couldn't help but wonder if Raylene had "seen" what someone wanted her to see.

Mr. Hornblower's gaze drifted as if revisiting old memories. "Danny had a rough life to be sure, but he had a lot of potential. If he hadn't disappeared, he would've been my nominee for the scholarship the Munks started in Joelle's memory."

"Congressman Munk's family commissioned the scholarship?"

"Yes, they were very generous to the school. As I recall, they'd financed all new uniforms for the football team the previous year."

The way Kaylee had heard it, there'd been an ulterior motive behind the "gift" of the uniforms. Could the same be true of the scholarship? Had the family started it to appease a guilty conscience?

Kaylee shook her head, hating that she'd automatically assumed the worst.

Mr. Hornblower purchased a bouquet of mixed gerberas for his daughter then left.

Jessica slipped in a few minutes later when Kaylee and Mary were freshening up displays. Jessica glanced down each aisle, then whispered, "Is the store empty?"

Kaylee chuckled at her cloak-and-dagger antics. "Yes. What's going on?"

"Joy Skenandore was just in my shop sampling my new

cinnamon-honey donuts, and she started reminiscing about how Ted's mother was the first one who brought cinnamon-flavored honey to the island. Apparently she'd been a hobby apiarist, supplying hives to local farmers when needed, and she created her own unique honey blends that were very popular at the Saturday morning farmers market."

"What does that have to do with—" Kaylee began, but then it hit her. "Oh, you think Ted might have acquired his mother's apiary skills and coaxed a couple of bees into Keith's car?"

"It's possible," Jessica said.

"Reese is working at the Munk house," Mary said. "You should ask him if Ted still has hives on the back of the property."

Maybe it was wishful thinking, but Kaylee had hoped Keith's bee encounter had truly been a coincidental accident. If her note writer would go so far as to try to take out Keith as well as Dwayne, what would stop him from doing the same to her?

"Oh, hold on." Jessica held up a hand. "I have an idea." She hurried out of the shop and returned a couple of minutes later with a bakery box. "You can take this to Reese for his lunch. Say it's a thank-you for helping with the flooded basement—and take a peek around the Munk property."

"I can tell Reese why I'm really there," Kaylee said.

"Sure, but this way if Ted's around, he doesn't have to know."

Mary tapped her index finger to her lips. "Are you sure it's a good idea to flaunt the man's competition in front of him? You know how tenacious he is about getting what he wants."

"Reese isn't his competition," Kaylee said.

"He should be." Jessica winked.

Kaylee relieved her of the box of donuts. "I meant I'm not interested in Ted. I'll stop around after I deliver Maeve Gilchrist's wedding order." She realized she had more news for her friends.

She updated them on her visit to Keith's last night. "Nick doesn't think he's guilty of anything, going by his body language. But I've got to admit, seeing all those newspapers bothered me."

"Then again," Jessica said, "if he'd sent you a note written in newsprint, he would've more likely avoided taking you to the room piled with old newspapers."

"True."

"What do you know about this Bob guy?" Mary asked. "You'd mentioned before that he seemed annoyed by your asking questions. Sounds like someone who might try to spook you into stopping."

Kaylee nodded. "Yeah, and he knew I was meeting Randy for dinner the night my tires were flattened. But other than his being a high school buddy of Keith's who now works for Neil's landscaping company, I don't know anything about him."

Mary reached under the counter and pulled out the old high school yearbook Reese had borrowed from the library for them. "What's his last name?"

"Mackey."

Mary flipped through the pages. "Here he is. He was a year behind Neil and Ted. Played on the football team. He would've known them that way."

Kaylee studied the team picture, then perused the candid photos on the facing page. "I can't imagine what motive he could have had. Of course anyone at that party could've had too much to drink and gone for an out-of-control joyride."

Mary glanced at her watch. "We should probably start loading the Gilchrist-Everett flowers into the van."

"I need to get back too," Jessica said. "Keep me posted on what you find out."

Twenty minutes later, Kaylee headed out with the wedding order. Three blocks later, her engine started knocking.

Her palms became slick with sweat. What if her note writer had gotten to the van? After what had happened to her personal vehicle last night, she sure didn't want to risk getting stranded somewhere, not to mention fail to deliver the flower arrangements.

Spotting Nelson's Mechanics Shop a block and a half away, she risked the distance and pulled into the parking lot.

An older gentleman who shared Raylene's cobalt-blue eyes walked out, wiping greasy hands on an even greasier rag. "I heard the engine knock as you pulled in. How long have you had that?"

"It just started."

"You were smart to bring it right in. Sounds as if your air-fuel mixture is off. If you let that go, it can cause damage to the piston and cylinder wall."

"Do you have time to look at it now? I have a flower order I need to deliver." She checked her watch. "If I can't get back on the road within the hour, I'll have to call someone."

"Shouldn't take long." He set the van to idle and picked up a bottle of something, which he dumped into the gas tank. Moments later, the knocking stopped. "That should take care of it."

Kaylee raised her eyebrows. "Really?"

"For now. When you have more time, bring it back for an overhaul. Your exhaust is a little smoky."

"I will. Thank you. What do I owe you?"

He waved off the question. "Don't worry about it."

"Wow, I appreciate it. You're a lifesaver." She started to climb into the van but paused. "I think I might've met your daughter the other day. Raylene?"

"Yes, that's our girl."

"I wondered. You have the same eyes."

"Yup. We're real proud of her."

"I guess this is where Congressman Munk brings his car then

too? He mentioned he had some trouble with his Mustang," she said, hoping he'd elaborate on the nature of the trouble.

The man laughed. "Ted's a hypochondriac when it comes to his car. We changed the oil and detailed it and it was good as new."

Mr. Nelson was either as good as his daughter at spinning a story . . . or Ted's bumper didn't need hammering out because he plowed into the back of Dwayne's car. Then again, would hitting a plastic bumper cause a dent in solid chrome?

"I wish they still made chrome bumpers like that on vehicles. I just tapped into a grocery cart and cracked mine," she said, hoping Mr. Nelson would take the bait.

"A tap like that wouldn't dent the old chrome bumpers."

In other words, the chances of her proving any of her theories about Ted's involvement were slim to none.

With another thank-you to Mr. Nelson, Kaylee went on her way. She delivered her order, then swung over to Ted's place. Reese's pickup was in the driveway, but not Ted's Mustang. *Perfect.* She grabbed the donut box and tracked the sound of hammering to the backyard. "Hey, you hungry?"

Reese grinned at the sight of her, or maybe the donut box. He set down his hammer and grabbed his water bottle. "What brings you here?"

"I had a flower delivery nearby, and Jess had a new donut recipe she thought you'd like." She opened the box and presented the choices to him.

"And?" he said, helping himself.

She grinned. "And I figured it'd give me a chance to snoop."

"You still think Ted is connected to Danny's death?"

"I don't know. It turns out Raylene was the witness who saw Danny at the harbor that night, which makes me suspicious. But all our evidence is circumstantial. By the same reasoning, it could be Keith."

"Except that Keith almost wound up dead."

"Yeah, and Jess said Ted could have beehives here." Kaylee craned her neck to peer to the back of Ted's yard.

"I don't think there are any bees in the hives anymore. I haven't seen any buzzing around."

Kaylee shrugged. "It was a long shot. At least you got some donuts out of the deal."

"Kaylee?" Ted's voice boomed from the corner of the house a second before he strode into view. "I thought that was your truck in the driveway. Good to see you."

"I was in the area," she said lamely.

"Well, come on in. I'll show you around."

"Shout if you need rescuing," Reese whispered, his eyes twinkling with amusement.

"I might take you up on that," she said before following Ted inside.

She wasn't sure what she expected. Opulence, she supposed. But the home's decor was surprisingly down-to-earth and, frankly, a bit dated. But she supposed that made sense, since he was rarely in residence there.

He motioned her into his den, where a stack of newspapers immediately snagged her attention. Not that she should be surprised to see a collection of national papers on a congressman's desk, whether he was vacationing or not. But that didn't stop her from experiencing a swell of nervous curiosity.

She sidled around the desk and glanced in the trash can. Empty. She slanted a sideways glance at the recycle bin tucked halfway into a cupboard. It was filled with newspapers, but none appeared to be cut, with the exception of a single large square that matched the clipped photo on his desk of him glad-handing at a Labor Day parade. She turned her attention to the rest of the room.

Trophies lined the shelves, and pictures of Ted holding them filled the wall around a golf club mounted in a long, narrow, glass-and-wood box. "A special club?" she asked.

He shot it a cursory glance. "It was my dad's idea."

"Why? What's special about it?"

"It's the driver I used to win my first junior club championship."

"Wow, I'm surprised you'd want to retire your lucky club."

He shrugged.

Kaylee read the nameplate beneath the club, dated the same year Danny disappeared. A coincidence?

"Here, let me show you the solarium." Ted pushed open the door on the far side of the room as Kaylee scrutinized the club's wooden head.

It was much smaller than that of the driver she'd borrowed from Mary. In fact, its size reminded her of the twin cracks on the back of Danny's skull. Her spine tingled at the sudden notion. Two separate blows from this club could've caused the cracks in Danny's skull. It was a more plausible scenario than the coroner's theory that he'd sustained multiple cracks by hitting his head on the broad well cap.

"Kaylee?" Ted said, interrupting her thoughts.

"The club's head looks a little splintered," she observed, and wondered if bits of lacquered wood could've survived being buried for thirty-five years.

"It happens. The solarium is this way." He motioned to the next room.

His eagerness to get her away from the club heightened her suspicions, but she dutifully followed, curbing the urge to take another gander at the club. Hiding a murder weapon in plain sight was an ingenious cover. And guys like Ted and his father were the kind of men with the audacity to do it.

"Would you like to stay for supper?" Ted asked.

"Thanks, but I can't. I already have plans." *Like trying to convince the sheriff to get a search warrant for your house.*

Ted's enthusiasm for the tour seemed to dwindle. After viewing the very impressive solarium, Kaylee said she'd better get back to the shop. Ted walked her to her delivery van.

Kaylee was pretty sure she could feel Reese's gaze on them.

"How's Mrs. Banks treating you?" Ted asked.

"Not bad." Kaylee hoped the question wasn't meant as a subtle reminder of how much she owed him. "I think I finally won her over with a wedding favor suggestion."

"Glad to hear it." He waved. "I'll see you around."

Kaylee drove straight to the sheriff's office, and Aida Friedman, the receptionist, waved her through to Maddox's office.

"Did the coroner happen to find any wood embedded in Danny's skull?" she asked as she came through the door.

The sheriff eyed her warily. "Why?"

"The damage to Danny's skull didn't look to me as if it resulted from landing on the broad topside of the well pipe."

"What do you think it came from?"

"A golf club. A driver to be exact."

"Did you find an old golf club lying around the flower shop's yard?"

"No, it's—" she squirmed, knowing he wasn't going to like what she had to say—"it's encased in glass at Ted Munk's house."

To her surprise, he laughed so hard his eyes watered. He swiped at them. "That's a good one. You had me going there for a second."

"I'm serious. What better place to dispose of a murder weapon than to hide it in plain sight?"

Maddox instantly sobered. "Let me get this straight. You think Congressman Munk killed Danny with a golf club?"

"Yes. Danny was a caddy for Ted's father and presumably was happy to do other things for him for the right price. Things like scuttle the boat of Ted's competition." Kaylee paused to gauge the sheriff's reaction. He started shaking his head, so she rushed on. "I figure Joelle's death was an accident, and either Ted was afraid Danny would turn him in and ruin them all, or Danny tried to blackmail him in return for keeping quiet."

Maddox tilted his head. "Yesterday you were trying to convince me Danny wouldn't have gone anywhere near a boat."

"That's true. It could be that Danny saw Ted or someone Ted hired ram the boat, and used that information to blackmail him."

The sheriff frowned at her. "I trust you haven't been spreading this rumor among your gardening gals. The congressman's aide would slap you with a libel suit so fast your head would spin."

"Couldn't you just test the club for traces of blood?"

"No. I have no probable cause—" He held up his hand to stop her protest. "Your theory is nothing more than conjecture. I have no interest in going on a witch hunt after the congressman."

"You do know that Raylene was the witness who put Danny at the scene? Raylene, who had a massive crush on Ted back then and who now has a cushy job with him."

"You're suggesting she fabricated her testimony?"

"Maybe. From what I hear, she was always helping him with his homework to try and win his favor. Why not lie for him?"

Maddox shook his head. "After working on a few cases for the Seattle police department, I would've thought you'd know how investigations work. You need evidence."

"Test the club and I think we'll have our evidence."

"Not going to happen."

She was about to mention the newspapers she'd seen there, but the stern look on the sheriff's face changed her mind. Jessica had been right. If they wanted to convict Danny's killer, they needed a confession.

20

Kaylee left the sheriff's office and arrived back at The Flower Patch at the same time Mary's husband pulled up in his truck. "Did you figure out what's wrong with my car?" Kaylee asked.

Herb climbed out of his pickup, his mouth set in a grim line. "Yeah, there was water in your gas tank. When did you last fill up?"

"Almost a week ago. You think I got bad gas?"

He shook his head. "Not if it's been in the tank that long." He produced a small memory card from his pocket. "I pulled this from your dash cam. I thought it might tell us who did it. It would've kept recording until the battery ran out of juice."

"You think someone deliberately put water in my tank?"

"The weather has been too moderate for it to be condensation. It's a good thing you were close to home."

Kaylee's pulse quickened. Had her note writer moved past dispensing warnings to taking action? "Could I have lost control of the vehicle?"

"No, it would've just died. But if you'd driven it much longer, you could've had thousands of dollars of damage to your engine."

Kaylee reeled at the news. She couldn't afford any more repair bills.

"Want to see the footage?" Herb motioned toward the shop's door.

"I sure do." Ted's bodyguard had been at the library last night, probably following her again. If the dash cam caught him sabotaging her car, it could be the evidence she needed to convince the sheriff to take a closer look at Ted.

DeeDee and Jessica were gathered around the counter with Mary as Kaylee and Herb walked in.

"What's going on?" Kaylee asked.

"I called them after Herb called me," Mary said.

Despite the grim situation, Kaylee smiled. "Thanks. You guys are the best."

Mary took the memory card from Herb and inserted it into the shop computer. A list of video files appeared on the screen.

"Try that one first." Kaylee pointed to the one from the previous night during the time she was at the library and then off with Nick, visiting Keith.

Mary double-clicked the file. The program for viewing videos opened, and everyone jockeyed for a clear view of the screen.

Kaylee fast-forwarded to the point she entered the library, then slowed it to merely triple time.

"Isn't that Chelsea?" Mary asked at the sight of Chelsea walking past the car.

"Yeah, with a couple of cousins in her wedding party." Kaylee paused the tape.

"What's that girl doing?" Jessica asked.

"Looks to me as if she's pointing out the car to someone outside the camera's view," DeeDee said.

Herb agreed.

Kaylee hit play at regular speed, and the girls moved out of the camera's view.

"Isn't that the deputy?" DeeDee asked when Nick paused and scrutinized Kaylee's car.

"Yeah, he was searching newspaper archives at the library." Kaylee glanced at the recorder's time—very close to when Nick joined her inside, not that she suspected him of sabotaging her car.

Jessica wagged her finger at the screen. "That's the black pickup that was following you."

Kaylee nodded. "Ted's bodyguard. I think he might still be trailing me."

On the video, the bodyguard looked through the windshield straight at the dash cam.

"Did you see that?" Herb asked. "He saw the camera."

"So if he put the water in your tank," Jessica said, "he would've made sure he didn't get caught on tape."

On screen, the retired teacher Kaylee had spoken to bustled past the front of the car carrying a bag of books, followed by the teen boy who'd been studying with Chelsea's cousin Eva.

"Wait," DeeDee said. "Rewind."

Kaylee did as instructed and everyone leaned closer to the screen.

"What's that kid carrying?" Mary asked.

"A water bottle," Jessica said.

"An empty water bottle," DeeDee clarified.

"A bottle he could've emptied into your gas tank." Jessica frowned at Kaylee. "Did you leave your car unlocked?"

Kaylee cringed. "Probably." As her grandfather used to say, it wasn't as if anyone could get very far if they tried to steal it. They were on an island. But she'd made it too easy for a would-be saboteur to pop the gas cover or the hood or whatever else they wanted to fiddle with.

"I don't recognize the kid," Herb said, which was saying a lot, since he'd been the town's mail carrier for years.

"I do," Jessica said. "He was in my shop with a group of high school students the day Reese brought in the yearbook for you."

Kaylee's breath hitched. She remembered the group. They'd been sitting at the table next to hers, which meant it wouldn't have been too difficult for one of them to slip something into her coffee—something that might've made her feel a lot sicker than she had, if she'd finished the whole cup. "Do you know who he is?"

DeeDee made a face. "He's the son of that new florist. He came into my bookstore yesterday asking for books on snakes, not realizing I stock mysteries. He said he keeps snakes as pets." DeeDee shook her head at the screen. "I'd gotten so caught up in thinking all the sabotage was from someone afraid you'd figure out they killed Danny, I missed the significance."

Mary gasped. "Of course."

"Of course what?" her husband asked.

"Don't you see? The new florist has been doing everything she can think of to try and derail our shop's business—slashing her prices, getting distant relatives to post nasty reviews."

Kaylee cocked her head to the side. "We don't know that was her."

"But it likely was," Mary said. "And I wouldn't put it past her kid to sneak in here and plant a snake in one of the pots to scare customers. The shop's front door was unlocked, remember?"

Kaylee squinted at the empty bottle in the boy's hand. "You might be right. I suppose he could've doused those plants with an acidic mix at the same time."

"And if he's a computer geek, he'd probably know how to send that anonymous e-mail," Jessica said, straightening.

Not wanting to believe her suspicions could've been so far off base, Kaylee continued to fast-forward through the tape, watching for Ted's bodyguard to return. Ted had admitted to paying him to watch her. Why not to sabotage her car? It wasn't as if she had concrete proof the teen poured the water from that bottle into her tank.

The bodyguard appeared on the screen, approaching from the direction of the library door, not the vehicle's tail end. He went directly to his vehicle and drove off.

Kaylee sighed. Finding out her competition instead of a murderer was harassing her should make her feel better, but it also meant she still didn't have answers about Danny for her grandmother. "What am I supposed to do now?"

"Talk to his mother," Herb said. "She probably has no idea what her son's been up to."

"You think?" Mary didn't seem so sure. "She might've put him up to the stuff. Or he could've learned by example."

"Maybe you could set up more cameras," DeeDee said. "Catch him definitively in the act so you can leave the hammering to the police."

"What if he does worse damage before then?" Jessica said. "You heard Herb. The water in the gas tank could've cost big bucks."

"He might've tweaked the air intake on my delivery van too," Kaylee said. "I had trouble with it today. And I think he was in the coffee shop the day I got queasy after that cup that tasted off. What if he spiked it with something nasty?"

"You definitely need to confront him then," DeeDee said. "Pretend the dash cam video caught him in the act and threaten to go to the police. He'll probably crack."

Jessica nodded. "That could work."

"Where do I confront him?" Kaylee asked.

"Nowhere near that cousin of Chelsea Banks," Mary said. "You don't want an unflattering account of it getting back to Mrs. Banks."

Kaylee shuddered at that thought.

"Let me do a little recon," Jessica said. "I'll see if I can find out where the new guy hangs out from some of the other teens who come to the shop." She headed back to Death by Chocolate. Less than a minute later, she texted Kaylee. *He's here now!*

Kaylee texted back. *I'll be right there.*

Mary flipped the shop sign to *Closed*. "We'll be right behind you."

Kaylee tucked her laptop under her arm and strode over

to Jessica's shop, reminding herself that she had needled the truth out of kids a lot smarter than this one during her stint as a college professor. Every semester, she'd find at least one student attempting to cheat his way through school, thinking she'd never find him out.

She pushed open the door and Jessica nodded at a table in the back. Kaylee recognized the boy from the library.

He glanced up.

Kaylee snagged his gaze and held it as she closed the distance between them.

His attention dropped to his drink, but she didn't miss his furtive peeks her way.

"Mind if I join you?" she asked, stopping in front of his table.

He stood. "You can have the table. I was just leaving."

DeeDee, Mary, and Herb flanked Kaylee.

"You have some explaining to do first," Herb said, his voice low and ominous.

The kid shrank back. "I don't know what you're talking about. You must have me confused with someone else."

"Nope." Kaylee took a seat at the teen's table and opened her laptop. "My dash cam got a clear picture of you and your water bottle."

His face paled.

"You might want to sit back down," Herb said.

This time, the kid obeyed.

"You're fortunate we caught onto your little prank before it damaged my car's engine, or you'd be looking at a steep bill in addition to a serious mischief charge." Kaylee gave him a stern gaze. "Why'd you do it?"

"I don't know."

Kaylee cocked her head, waiting for him to make eye contact once more. "Do we need the sheriff to talk to you and help you figure it out? Because I'm thinking your mom wouldn't appreciate that kind of publicity. I can see the headline now. 'Son of island's newest florist sabotages car of competition.'"

"I'm sorry. It was a stupid thing to do."

"You've got that right. So was the snake, the spiked coffee, and the killer plant fertilizer," she said, as if she knew for a fact he was behind them too.

He ducked his head, confirming her suspicions.

"How'd you get into my shop?"

He glanced up. "I didn't break in." He dropped his gaze once more. "The side door was unlocked."

"What did you put in the coffee?" Mary asked.

"It wasn't poison," he said, no longer trying to deny the accusations. "It was ipecac. Just a couple of drops."

"Ipecac? No wonder I felt like throwing up," Kaylee said.

"What's ipecac?" DeeDee asked.

"It's a syrup derived from rhizomes," Kaylee explained. "It used to be the default treatment to induce vomiting when a child accidentally ingested poison." She turned back to the teen. "What possessed you to do these things?"

"I like it here. I don't want to have to move again."

Kaylee crossed her arms. "So you figured you'd derail your mom's competition and life would be a bed of roses?"

He gulped. "Yeah, something like that."

"What's your name?"

"Greg. Greg Simmons."

"Well, Greg, we're talking trespassing and property damage, and I'm pretty sure the judge would consider those notes threats."

Greg's head snapped up. "What notes? I didn't write any notes."

Kaylee's insides churned. She stared him down, the same way she used to scrutinize her college students, but his expression was open and shocked. "The note at my house? The e-mail?"

He vigorously shook his head. "I swear I didn't send any e-mails or notes."

"What about the flat tires?"

A mix of confusion and fear clouded his features. "I didn't do anything to your tires either."

Kaylee realized that she believed him. Which meant someone else out there really did want to make sure she stopped asking questions about Danny.

"Are you going to call the cops?" Greg asked.

"That depends," Kaylee said. "Are you done sabotaging my business?"

Sweat beaded on his forehead. "Yes, I swear. I won't do anything else."

She decided to take a page from her grandmother's book. "All right. You can pay off the damages by working in the yard tomorrow. It needs raking and reseeding where it had to be dug up to fix the well. And there's always weeding to be done."

"I usually help my mom on Saturdays."

"Well, I'd be happy to talk to her and explain why—"

"No! I'll be here."

"Good. I'll see you at nine o'clock sharp."

"Okay." Greg scrambled out of the shop like a frightened mouse.

DeeDee chuckled. "Well, that's one mystery solved."

"Sure," Mary said. "But someone out there still doesn't want us asking questions about Danny's death."

21

At five minutes to nine the next morning, Kaylee peered up and down the street for Greg, wishing she'd asked him to come before the shop opened so she could get him started on his work before any customers showed up.

A bike rounded the corner of Pacific Street a block down, the rider pedaling like mad.

Kaylee squinted and breathed a relieved sigh when she recognized Greg. She carried out the tools she'd gathered and met him in the yard. "Glad to see you made it."

He propped his bike against the fence. "I'm sorry for what I did," he said, without meeting her eyes.

She figured he was more sorry about getting caught, but hoped a hard day's work would convince him not to pull any more foolish stunts. She handed him a pair of work gloves and a rake. "First thing I want you to do is rake smooth this area that's been dug up. Then you can evenly sprinkle the grass seed from the bucket over the whole area."

"That's it?" he said, sounding hopeful.

"Nope. Then you can rake up the fallen leaves and put them in the compost pile in the back corner, and you can weed the flower beds. When you've finished all of that, I'll bring out a sprinkler you can set up to water the grass seed. Any questions?"

"When's my break?"

Kaylee narrowed her eyes. "You can rest when you need to. But a fit young man like yourself should be able to work at least a couple of hours steady before needing a break. Don't you think?"

He shrugged. "I guess."

"Good." She set the rest of the tools next to the flower bed. "If you need anything else, just knock on that window"—she pointed to the one closest to the showroom—"and I'll come out as soon as I can get away. Okay?"

"Yeah."

She rounded the shop to go through the front door and missed a step at the sight of Bob.

He jumped down from his pickup truck and slammed the door. "Me and you need to have a talk."

She glanced up and down the street, hoping Bob's confrontational tone wouldn't scare away any customers, because she sure didn't feel like inviting him inside.

"Keith says you been asking questions about me."

Kaylee nodded. *Yup, should've seen that one coming.* "Why don't you like me?"

The question seemed to take him aback for a moment. "It's what you're doing I don't like."

"And what is it you think I'm doing?"

"Asking questions. Stirring up grief that don't need stirring up."

"You mean grief over Joelle's death?"

"Yeah. My mom was in the coffee shop the afternoon you and your cronies were speculating over who rammed Neil's boat, if it wasn't Danny."

"And the first thing she did was call to warn you?" Kaylee swallowed, as the obvious implication struck her. Suddenly she wished the street weren't quite so deserted this morning.

"You bet. As soon as she heard someone mention Neil. Let me tell you, Neil's never got past feeling guilty for not being with Joelle that night. The last thing he needs is a bunch of busybodies getting the whole town talking about it all over again."

"And where were you that night?"

He scowled at her. "Why don't you ask what you really want to know?"

She searched his eyes and somehow already knew the answer. "I'm sorry."

Her apology seemed to take the wind out of his blustering. He acknowledged her apology with a nod. "And just so you know," he said in a less menacing tone, "I arrived at the party with Keith and never left until after we heard about Joelle's accident." Moisture filled his eyes. He took a moment to gather himself, then asked, "You really think Danny didn't do it?"

She sighed. "It doesn't add up. My grandmother says he was afraid to go out on the water. But others have suggested that was a lie. His so-called accidental death, which made it look as if he ran, just seems too conveniently coincidental."

Bob seemed to contemplate her perspective with a new one of his own. "You might be right. Well, if it wasn't Danny who killed Joelle, I hope you find the—"

"Thank you for stopping by," Kaylee said brightly over Bob's rather colorful description of Joelle's killer, hoping to prevent arriving customers from hearing it.

He actually grinned. "I'll see you around."

The morning flew by, thanks to a steady stream of customers, but that didn't spare her from thoughts about who had sent the note and the e-mail—and likely silenced Dwayne. Nick seemed certain Glen couldn't have been responsible for Dwayne's accident, and Glen's arthritic hands made it unlikely he'd cut and paste letters. So if it wasn't Bob, Keith, Neil, or Joelle's father, that left Ted Munk as her prime suspect.

He had been in the coffee shop the morning she and the Petals had batted around theories about Danny being murdered, less than a day before Bear found the note. A note Ted certainly had access to enough newspapers to create. Besides, he could have commissioned Raylene to do it for him. And as a congressman, his Internet activity was probably all on a VPN. Not to mention that of all the suspects, she knew without a doubt that he had seen her with Dwayne. And felt the need to have his bodyguard watch her.

But Sheriff Maddox had made it abundantly clear that he wouldn't investigate the congressman without hard evidence.

So what was she supposed to tell her grandmother? Somehow Kaylee was pretty sure it wouldn't make Bea feel any better to learn that another of her employees was Kaylee's prime suspect.

A hard rap on the window made her jump. Bear, who was on his dog bed nearby, raised his head at her sudden movement. He must have assumed nothing was really amiss, as he rested his head on his paws to continue his nap. She turned to the window and determined the cause of the noise—Greg.

"You bringing out that sprinkler?" he shouted through the glass.

She gave him a thumbs-up. "Be out in a minute."

"I'm going to grab a snack next door. Be right back."

Kaylee descended into the basement and grabbed the sprinkler off the bench in the corner. Spinning around to head back up the stairs, she jumped at the sight of Ted Munk coming down them. "Congressman, what are you doing here?"

"I'm heading back to the mainland today. I'm afraid this is goodbye."

Kaylee swallowed hard. "It was a pleasure meeting you. Grandma was sorry she missed you this year."

A reflective expression flitted across his face. "She was the best boss I ever had. It's unfortunate this business with remains in the yard had to sully our getting to know each other."

Kaylee's heart thumped. Did he know she suspected him of being involved? Was that why he was really here? He stood three steps from the bottom, blocking the only way out of the basement.

Greg would be back in the yard soon. Surely the congressman wouldn't try anything with a potential witness around. If he'd noticed him, that is.

"Grandma was heartbroken to hear it was Danny." Kaylee set down the water sprinkler and picked up the closest weapon at hand—the rusty breaker bar. "She blames herself."

"I'm sorry to hear that."

"She needs to know what really happened."

"She needs to let it go. Danny was the kind of kid who was always trying to find an angle to play. If he hadn't fallen in that hole, it would've been something else that got him."

"I know you two fought. What happened? Did he threaten to blackmail you?"

Ted's eyebrows rose ever so slightly, but he didn't seem all that surprised by her question. "Dwayne tell you that?"

"I figured Danny confronted you around the eighteenth tee."

Ted nodded. "He was talking crazy. He said he *knew* I killed Joelle. Claimed he saw my boat out there and said he wanted 100 grand to disappear. I laughed at him."

"What did he do?" Kaylee's heart was practically pounding out of her chest. The man was giving her a confession, which could only mean one thing, according to Mary—he planned to kill her too. Her palms grew slick. She tightened her grip on the breaker bar. If she stalled Ted long enough, Greg would come looking for her. Or a customer would come in. The shop was strangely quiet for a Saturday. What if he had turned the shop sign to *Closed*?

"Danny jumped the fence into the Spieces' yard. Threatened to tell Joelle's dad then and there that I rammed her boat."

"Is that when you hit him with your golf club?"

"What? No." He gaped at her.

She kept talking, trying to stall him. "Sheriff Maddox knows about the golf club. Blood is almost impossible to completely clean off. They have chemicals that will—"

"I didn't hit him with my golf club!" Ted roared. He tightened his fist, visibly working at lowering his voice. "Yes, I have a temper, but I never killed the kid. I hopped the fence and pounded him for spouting lies about me. We wrestled on the ground for a bit, which could be when he picked up that pinecone you found. But he was alive when I hopped back over the fence and played out my last hole."

"Weren't you worried people would believe him if he talked?"

Ted made a dismissive noise. "Not a chance. I was at a party that night. Almost my entire class would've vouched for me."

"So why send me the notes? Were you afraid your classmates' memories would be fuzzy after all these years?"

He frowned. "I didn't send you any notes."

She studied him a long time. He looked genuinely bewildered. "You saw me with Dwayne, and three hours later his car was wrapped around a tree. The next morning, yours was in the shop, and an e-mail was in my in-box with a photograph of the accident and a warning that this was what happens to people who don't heed warnings."

"It wasn't from me. Did it say it was?"

"No." Kaylee mentally reviewed all the evidence that seemed to point to Ted. Keith had a collection of mainland newspapers in his house that he could've easily made the note from too. Could she have been wrong about his old buddy Bob this morning? He could've seen her talking to Dwayne and taken care of him for Keith.

Another image nudged into Kaylee's memory: Raylene watching them play golf from the clubhouse's veranda. Had she still been there by the time they finished the game? Keeping an eye on Kaylee while Ted changed? Ensuring Kaylee didn't do anything that might jeopardize Ted's run for governor?

As Ted's assistant, or whatever she considered herself, she would've had unfettered access to those newspapers at his house too. DeeDee had said cut-and-paste notes were a woman's MO. Raylene probably thought she was protecting Ted from potential negative press. Maybe she even believed he'd rammed Joelle's boat all those years ago. She had told investigators she'd seen Danny at the harbor that night. Had her testimony merely been another attempt on her part to win Ted's favor? Bea had mentioned Raylene had a crush on him.

Kaylee's heart jolted at another thought. What if Raylene had overheard what Dwayne had said about Danny coming into money? She'd have been worried the press would get the story and start digging. Maybe worried enough to silence Dwayne herself.

A cold shiver trickled down Kaylee's spine. Raylene was a mechanic's daughter and likely had the know-how to drain Dwayne's brakes, not to mention to fiddle with the air intake on the shop's delivery van. "Who did you tell about Danny's blackmail threat at the time?" Kaylee asked Ted.

He frowned. "No one."

"You didn't tell your father?"

"No. I may have had a little too much to drink that night, but I wasn't stupid enough to pilot a boat in that condition and Danny knew it. So I didn't figure he'd have the guts to try the scheme on my dad."

"What about Raylene?" Kaylee glanced down at the breaker bar she'd picked up. It was exactly the kind of weapon a mechanic's daughter might find at hand in her father's truck to take care of the guy blackmailing her dream boyfriend—and could've accidentally dropped when Mr. Fitzpatrick yelled out his windows at would-be prowlers. Kaylee's heart pounded in her ears like the relentless surf. If her grandmother had found it in the yard some time later, she'd have just chalked it up to another of her grandfather's forgotten tools left lying about. "Did you mention Danny's threat to Raylene?" Kaylee repeated.

Ted shrugged. "Maybe. She was always helping me with my homework, so we talked a lot."

"Did you two ever date?"

"Raylene?" Ted's tone implied the idea was ridiculous. "No, it was never like that."

The landing at the top of the stairs creaked and Kaylee glanced up.

Raylene stood there watching them with eyes narrowed in a glare.

How much had she heard?

Raylene's gaze dropped to the breaker bar Kaylee held, and her lips twisted into a grimace. "Congressman, the ferry's about to leave. You'd better hurry."

"Right." He started up the stairs with Kaylee two steps behind him, then suddenly paused as something on her grandfather's old workbench caught his attention. "No way. Is that a Mustang hood ornament?" He darted past Kaylee down the stairs.

The door at the top clicked shut.

Kaylee's blood ran cold.

As Ted hurried to the workbench, Kaylee continued to climb the stairs, doing her best to appear unconcerned by Raylene's looming stance. Ted let out an appreciative whistle. "This is vintage. I've been trying to find one of these for years. Would you consider selling it?"

Kaylee glanced from the object in Ted's hand to Raylene still blocking the exit with her gaze fixed on Kaylee.

"You're welcome to have it," Kaylee said brightly, closing the distance between her and Raylene to a few steps.

Raylene pulled a gun. "Sorry, that's as far as you're going," she said in a hiss. "Now drop the breaker bar."

"In your dreams." Kaylee swung it with all her might at Raylene's gun.

The woman's leg snapped up and her foot clipped the bar, sending it toppling to the cellar floor.

"Whoa." Ted jumped back, still holding his precious find. "Watch where you're tossing that."

The door at the top of the stairs burst open. "Kaylee? Are you down there?" It was George.

"Call the sheriff!" Kaylee shouted. "Don't come down here."

"What? Why?" He stepped onto the landing.

Raylene spun around and clocked him on the head with her gun, and he crumpled at her feet.

22

Kaylee lurched toward George.

Raylene aimed her gun at Kaylee's chest. "Stay where you are." Raylene waited until Kaylee straightened, hands raised in surrender. "Back to the wall."

Kaylee shifted on the step and Raylene used her foot to shove George's crumpled body down the stairs past Kaylee.

"Raylene? What are you doing?" Ted dropped to his knee at George's side and felt his pulse.

"What I always do. Cleaning up your messes." Raylene tossed Ted a rope. "Tie him up."

"Have you lost your mind?" Ted's tone was incredulous. "He's unconscious. He needs a doctor." Ted snatched up a nearby rag and pressed it to George's bleeding head.

Kaylee scanned the basement for some way to subdue Raylene.

"Did he see you?" Raylene demanded of Ted.

"I don't know. What does it matter? Where did you get that gun? What has gotten into you?"

Raylene spared him only a brief steely glance. "Forget the rope and move her upstairs before he comes to. Someone will find him eventually."

"We can't just leave him," Kaylee said.

Raylene sneered. "Trust me. It's better than the alternative." She turned sideways on the landing and motioned Kaylee up the stairs with the gun. "Now move."

"Where are we going?" Kaylee planted her feet on the step where she stood and tried to picture what was near the door at the top. She couldn't outrun a bullet, but maybe she could slam the door and use something to hold it shut long enough for her to get away.

"We're going for a little ride," Raylene snarled.

"Now wait a minute." Ted released the compress he'd been holding to George's head and stood. "This has gone too far. I told Kaylee I didn't kill Danny. She's not going to drag my name through the mud. Maddox has closed the case. There's nothing to spin here."

"You really think she believes you?" Raylene scoffed. "At least you were smart enough to leave your car by the harbor. I don't think anyone saw you slip in the back door."

Kaylee started up the stairs—slowly so as not to distract them from their argument—and silently prayed George would be okay.

"Why wouldn't she believe me?" Ted asked incredulously. "It's the truth."

"Trust me," Raylene said. "People aren't interested in the truth."

Kaylee surged past Raylene on the landing and burst through the door.

It slammed closed behind her of its own accord.

Kaylee's heart all but jumped out of her chest.

"What on earth is going on here?" Mrs. Banks demanded.

Where did she come from? Kaylee would have rolled her eyes if she hadn't been trying to escape a killer. Instead, she rammed the basement door's flimsy slide bolt closed, for what good it would do. "Run!"

"Your front door's locked," Mrs. Banks blathered on, oblivious to the danger. "If I hadn't seen the plumber enter at the back—"

"Watch out!" Kaylee yanked over the wall display unit nearest the basement door.

Mrs. Banks jerked back, but not fast enough to escape the vases crashing to the floor. One pinged her shoulder and sent her toppling into the narrow hallway's opposite wall.

Ted or Raylene rammed the door.

Kaylee grabbed Mrs. Banks by the elbow.

"Have you lost your mind?" the woman screeched. "What are you doing barricading that poor man down there?"

Kaylee hauled the woman to her feet. "We need to get out of here. Now."

"Kaylee, wait!" Ted shouted through the door, followed by a hard shove that rattled the frame. "This is all a misunderstanding."

Mrs. Banks yanked Kaylee to a halt. "That's Congressman Munk! Why have you locked the congressman in your basement?"

A gunshot splintered the door.

"That's why!" Kaylee grabbed Mrs. Banks's arm and raced for the front door.

Footsteps stormed behind them.

Kaylee fumbled to release the front door's lock, but it was jammed.

"Freeze," Raylene ordered, "Or you'll end up like the congressman."

What? Kaylee stilled and agonizing moans broke through the roar of blood rushing past her ears. She slowly turned, and at the sight of Ted clutching his bleeding chest, her stomach roiled. "You shot him? Why?"

Raylene's voice turned saccharine. "Because you found out his dirty little secret and there was no way he could let you live. But how could I live with myself if I let him get away with another murder? A girl can only rescue a guy so many times."

"Before she finally has to accept he's never going to appreciate her the way she wants him to," Kaylee finished.

Raylene smirked. "I knew you were a smart one."

Mrs. Banks gaped at Kaylee. "The congressman tried to kill you?"

Rushing to Ted's side, Kaylee exchanged a glance with Raylene. Her message, silent but threatening, was clear—if Kaylee played along with Raylene's spin on the situation, Mrs. Banks might get to live. Kaylee stripped the tulle off a nearby display and pressed it to the congressman's bleeding chest.

He moaned at her touch, but never opened his eyes.

"He didn't want me spreading rumors implicating him in Danny Lane's death," Kaylee said quietly. That much was true at least.

Mrs. Banks gasped, then covering her mouth with her hand, stared wide-eyed at Ted. "To think I voted for the man."

Seemingly satisfied the woman had been duped, Raylene shifted her gun's aim to Ted, now in conveniently close proximity to Kaylee.

Kaylee snuck a peek out the store's front window. Had no one heard the gunshot? She blanched as she remembered Greg. What if he walked in on Raylene holding a gun? *Oh Lord, please let him be still getting his snack. Or better yet, getting help.*

She flailed about for a new plan. If Ted didn't get medical attention ASAP, he wouldn't live long enough to clear his name and ensure Raylene—the real culprit—paid for everything she'd done. And might still do.

Something hard bumped against Kaylee's knee. Ted's phone. He'd surreptitiously muted the volume and pressed 9, before edging it toward her. Keeping it hidden from Raylene's view, Kaylee finished entering 911 and hit the dial icon.

"The sheriff is on his way," Raylene said, apparently for Mrs. Banks's benefit because Kaylee knew it was a lie.

She snuck another glance at Ted's phone. *The call connected!* "You told them to come to The Flower Patch?" Kaylee asked loudly, hoping the dispatcher would hear.

Raylene's gaze narrowed on Kaylee.

She shifted, nudging the phone under the small of Ted's back with her knee, and silently prayed the dispatcher would still be able to hear.

Raylene motioned to Mrs. Banks. "Why don't you run upstairs and find some towels to stop the bleeding? And maybe a blanket."

Mrs. Banks scurried to do her bidding.

The moment she cleared the stairs, Ted kicked. His foot caught Raylene's shin, before his leg flopped uselessly to the floor.

Raylene scarcely flinched. "Hurts to lose, doesn't it, Congressman? Not that I wanted you to. I did everything I could to stop this. To ensure you'd win. But you were as clueless as ever." She stooped at his other side as Kaylee continued to hold pressure on his wound. "But I'm glad to see you still have some fight in you. Just enough, I daresay, to take out the woman who could ruin you." She pressed the gun into his limp hand and aiming it toward Kaylee, wrapped her fingers around his. *Her gloved fingers.*

"Why did you kill Joelle?" Kaylee blurted. Her gaze bounced from the gun's trigger to Raylene's face. She needed to stall for time, and she'd read somewhere that, deep down, murderers yearned to confess and receive credit for their deeds.

A skin-crawling smile curved Raylene's lips. "What makes you think I did?" she said, neither confirming nor denying, but looking impressed by the question.

"You loved Ted and you wanted him to love you. That's why you let him copy your homework in high school."

She chuckled. "And why I told the sheriff I saw Danny near the boats that night. It wasn't a lie."

Pain flickered across Ted's face.

Kaylee gathered more tulle from the nearby display and pressed it to his still-seeping wound, wishing she had a fabric with more substance at hand. "But you didn't say it to cover for Ted, did you?"

She lifted her shoulders in a noncommittal shrug. "Ted's dad saw the red paint on his boat and feared the worst. He buffed it off so the sheriff wouldn't find it. And my eyewitness account got Ted out of trouble with his dad."

"I imagine Mr. Munk was grateful."

"Naturally."

"Not like Ted. I'm guessing he still scarcely noticed you at the party that night. Is that why you went out in their boat, Raylene? You figured you'd take a joyride and he'd never miss you?" Just like Eva had done last Sunday at the park with Matt's bike.

Raylene's gaze turned to steel and Kaylee's breath caught. Had she pushed too hard?

"I did him a favor. He couldn't have beaten Neil in that upcoming race."

"You killed Joelle just so Ted could win a race?"

"I merely squeezed the boat toward the rocks. It was a whim. She wasn't supposed to fall out." Raylene's gaze drifted with the recollection. "Joelle freaked and cranked it too hard. She scraped Ted's boat, then a rock. The next thing I knew, her boat capsized. I tried to save her, but she wasn't wearing a life jacket. I raced back to shore for help, but when I realized it was too late . . . well, self-preservation kicked in."

Kaylee's heart thundered at Raylene's admission. She hoped the dispatcher was getting every word.

"No one saw me return, so I docked the boat and kept quiet. It was two weeks to graduation. I was heading to college, then law school. Why ruin the rest of my life over an accident?"

"But Danny's death wasn't an accident. Was it?" Out of the corner of her eye, Kaylee spotted Mrs. Banks frozen at the top of the stairs. *Please, please, please, don't let Raylene see her.*

Raylene snorted. "Danny got greedy. He knew he was innocent, so he figured Ted was guilty and threatened to blackmail him. I couldn't let him get away with that."

"So you lured him to the flower shop?"

"He didn't know what hit him. Twice."

Mrs. Banks gasped.

Raylene startled, apparently having forgotten about the other woman. Her hand tightened around Ted's on the gun.

Kaylee dove for cover.

Ted must've rallied and fought against Raylene's aim because the shot went wild, pinging the light fixture in the ceiling.

A hair-raising shriek rang out and Mrs. Banks charged down the stairs, wielding one of the heavy brass candlesticks the shop rented out for weddings.

Raylene swung the gun in Mrs. Banks's direction.

Mrs. Banks whacked Raylene's raised arm with a home-run swing that sent the gun flying.

"Way to go!" Kaylee jumped up and tackled Raylene before she could recover the gun. Kaylee pinned Raylene's face to the floor then wrenched her arms behind her back.

"Let me have another swing at her," Mrs. Banks said, breathless.

Laughter bubbled up Kaylee's chest at Mrs. Banks's warrior stance. Her country club clan would never recognize the fierce Amazon who stood before her.

"The place is surrounded!" Sheriff Maddox bellowed from outside, his voice amplified by a bullhorn. "Come out with your hands up."

"You better go out and tell them we have the bad guys subdued before they toss a can of tear gas in on us," Kaylee said to Mrs. Banks.

"Oh dear. Yes." Mrs. Banks bustled to the front door, still clutching the candlestick. She dropped it to fiddle with the lock, then hurried outside with her arms raised. "It's okay. We caught them. We need handcuffs and paramedics."

A deputy rushed forward and hurried the woman away from the building, then what had to be every other deputy on the island surged into the shop through every entrance. Several approached Kaylee and Raylene, while others went off to secure the building.

"George needs medical attention in the basement," Kaylee said. "He got knocked out and fell down the stairs. Ted's been shot in the chest. The gun's over there." She jutted her chin in the direction the gun had slid. Raylene squirmed beneath her and Kaylee yanked her arms further up her back. "Knock it off. It's over, Raylene. Sheriff, I could use a pair of handcuffs here. This is Raylene Nelson. She assaulted George, shot Ted, tried to kill me, held us hostage, and—"

"Killed Joelle and Danny," Sheriff Maddox finished, relieving Kaylee of Raylene's custody. "We heard. Good work."

The deputies declared the shop all clear and signaled for the paramedics.

Reese rushed in behind the EMTs. "Kaylee?"

"I'm fine," she said as a deputy stopped Reese before he could contaminate the scene. Two other officers caught Jessica, Mary, and DeeDee racing in behind him. Kaylee glanced around. "But where's Bear?" Panic gripped her. "Have you seen Bear?"

"He's in my truck," Reese said. "He ran all the way to where I was working and barked at me. That's how I knew something was wrong. Some watchdog, huh?"

Tears filled Kaylee's eyes. Raylene must have locked Bear out when she came in. Kaylee was grateful that's all she'd done.

The deputy who had hustled Mrs. Banks to safety returned with Bear cuddled in his arms. "Mrs. Banks refused to sit down and answer my questions until we brought this little guy in to see you. He was frantically clawing at the truck's windows."

Bear barked and wagged his tail at Kaylee.

The deputy set him down and Bear scampered to her. She scooped him into her arms and hugged him tight. "My hero."

It was Monday afternoon before the police finally released the crime scene and Kaylee was able to get back into the flower shop to clean up the bloodstains and fingerprint dust and shattered vases and toppled display case. But with Reese and Mary's help, the shop was shipshape in a couple of hours so that Kaylee could open as usual Tuesday morning.

Mrs. Banks strode in three minutes after Kaylee unlocked the front door. "How are you doing, dear? What a trauma you've been through."

Kaylee suppressed a smile at the woman's friendly tone. Apparently she'd finally won her over. "I'm doing great, thanks to your quick thinking Saturday. That was an impressive swing you had."

Mrs. Banks's cheeks turned pink and she actually giggled. "I played in a softball league in college. I guess it's kind of like riding a bike—comes right back to you."

Kaylee set aside the ribbons she'd been sorting. "How may I help you? Did you have a new idea for Chelsea's wedding?"

She waved a hand. "No, whatever you come up with will be gorgeous, I'm sure."

Kaylee gaped, speechless at the woman's uncharacteristic confidence in her.

"In fact," Mrs. Banks added, rummaging through her designer handbag, "I was thinking that with all these nasty setbacks you've had, you could probably use the full payment in advance." She pulled out a check. "Here." She handed it to Kaylee.

"Wow, thank you. That's so thoughtful."

She flapped a hand as if the gesture were nothing. "Did you hear the congressman is being released from the hospital today?

He can't say enough good things about you and how you saved his life. There was another interview about it in this morning's paper." Mrs. Banks beamed proudly.

Ah, the power of good publicity. "I'm happy Ted's recovered enough to be released. Poor George broke his leg tumbling down the stairs and got a nasty concussion. The doctor says it'll be a few more weeks before he'll be up and about." Kaylee smiled at the memory of how much he'd appreciated the cupcakes she'd taken him Sunday afternoon to cheer him up. She felt horrible that the only reason he'd shown up Saturday and gotten caught in the middle of her confrontation with Raylene was because he hadn't wanted to make her wait several more days for hot water.

"Thank goodness he arrived when he did," Mrs. Banks said, "or who knows what might have happened. Your grandmother must be very proud of how well you handled yourself. Not to mention that you solved two thirty-five-year-old murders!"

Kaylee nodded. "She's delighted that the lies about Danny have been proven false and that the real perpetrator will finally pay for her crimes."

"Oh yes, the poor congressman." Mrs. Banks adopted a sympathetic tone. "Such an embarrassment to him. But at least we can be confident he'll push for the full weight of the law to be brought to bear on her." The doorbell jingled and Mrs. Banks glanced over at the throng of well-heeled women that entered. She wiggled her fingers in their direction, then grinned at Kaylee. "And it looks like business is starting to pick up."

Kaylee returned the smile, feeling fairly confident that Mrs. Banks was quite right about that—especially when the older woman approached the newcomers and said, "Ladies, you have absolutely come to the right place. Kaylee Bleu can handle anything you throw at her."

Don't miss the Secrets of the Castleton Manor Library!

Join Faith Newberry and her cat, Watson, in the quaint town of Lighthouse Bay on Cape Cod in Massachusetts as she marries her love of books to a penchant for sleuthing. After landing her dream job as librarian at Castleton Manor, an upscale literary retreat, Faith is forced to read between the lines and solve the mysteries she finds among the stacks. Faith, Watson, and the lively members of the Candle House Book Club set out to unravel whodunits that might have stumped even Sherlock Holmes. Enjoy the thrill of the hunt with Faith and her friends as they solve puzzling crimes, discover dark secrets, and embrace heartwarming truths that have long been hidden in the voluminous pages of the Castleton Manor Library.

Learn more at AnniesFiction.com!